The Return To Treasure Island

Also by Raymond Barnett:

Jade and Fire

Relax, You're Already Home

The China Ultimatum

The Return To TREASURE ISLAND

A novel by
RAYMOND BARNETT

www.raymondbarnett.com

Cover and illustrations by Sarena Kirk

iUniverse, Inc.
Bloomington

I have gone off in search of a little adventure.

–Michael Chabon, *Gentlemen of the Road*, 2007

Chrysalis: ***the hardened structure in which a caterpillar undergoes transformation into a butterfly, by a process most ingenious, but poorly understood.***

–Samuel Johnson, Lexicographer and Critic, *circa* 1756

Table of Contents

Chapter One. Meilu. Shanghai, China, Spring 1756

My stomach was tight, and hurting, as the huge burnished door came into view. *Help me, Ma Tsu*, I prayed, squeezing the porcelain figure of the sea-goddess in my pocket. *I need your sea-strength. Help me live through this visit to Shanghai's richest mansion to claim my family's heritage, lost for three centuries.*

I quickly jerked the cord beside the door–before I lost my courage.

A slot opened, high up. Black eyes peered down at me. I shoved my hand at the eyes, the old ring showing prominent on my finger.

The eyes swept the hand contemptuously, pulled back to leave, then suddenly noticed the ring, peered closer, and opened wide. After a long stare, the slot snapped shut, and the door opened.

He was the biggest man I had ever seen. A broad, flat forehead, and curiously long arms. The way my tutor had described the Tanka, the boat people from another land used by the Black Pans who live in this mansion.

"I would see your master, about the ring," I said, in a quavering voice into which I willed courage. I was here from halfway around the world, and would not easily cast aside my quest.

He led me through halls rich with ebony and jade furnishings, to a smaller room, bamboo books lining the walls. A huge painting of an old man towered behind an ebony desk, looking a lot like my grandfather, except for the hint of weakness and cruelty around the mouth. A crimson phoenix flared on his gown, as on the cream carpet on the floor.

I sat on the edge of a long couch, alone in the room now. My tutor had said they were as likely to kill me as listen to me. I glanced toward the floor-length windows across the room, which opened onto the garden. That would be my way out, should I need to leave quickly.

The door opened. A tall woman in a golden silk gown shuffled into the room on tiny feet, supported on the arm of a young man. She was stunningly beautiful, in a formal sort of way, as if her beauty was painted onto her. Her age was impossible to guess, but her hair was jet black, with pieces of jade woven into it. The woman sat heavily in the chair behind the desk, while the young man remained standing, glowering at me.

"What is this about a ring?" she abruptly hissed, her voice soft but menacing.

I rose, and walked to the desk, raising my hand to her face.

"Give it to my son," she said peevishly, turning her head from my hand. "The ring interests me, not your dirty hand."

Reluctantly, I removed the ring and dropped it in the outstretched hand of the young man, who relayed it to his mother.

She breathed slowly as she peered closely at it. Tilted it toward the windows to catch more light. Turned it slowly around in her hand. Then gingerly placed it on the desk, beside a black stone inkwell with bamboo brushes resting on it.

"Where did you steal this ring?" she demanded, in the same low hiss.

"It was given me by my father, who received it from his father," I answered evenly. "Through centuries, it has been passed down in our family, a treasured heirloom from our great ancestor, Pan Fulong."

"*Do not say that name*!" The command erupted from her painted mouth like flame from a blaze. "The man whose ring and name you claim left China over three hundred years ago, early in the Ming dynasty," the woman spat out. "He sailed away in the great fleet of the emperor's eunuch,

Zheng He, and has not been seen–or heard of–since. So you see, what you say is preposterous."

"Yet I have the ring," I stubbornly pointed out. "Handed down with tales of its original owner, an accomplished navigator, captain of a ship like a city, which sailed from a faraway homeland, only to founder on the shoals north of our island, called by us Cuba. The survivors prospered on the island, until barbarians and their diseases arrived, and now we are reduced to my grandfather–the seeming twin of the man in that picture–and myself, sent here to discover who we are."

"Nonsense! Errant nonsense!" the old woman exploded. She motioned for the young man to come closer to her. "My son. Have you ever heard of this, this 'Cuba' she prattles on about?"

He whispered in her ear, but I could hear. "Never, Honored Mother. But the eunuch Zheng He spoke of many islands the Yong Le Emperor's fleet visited near the great continent Fusang in the eastern ocean."

She glared at me for a long moment, weighing it.

"How did you get here, to Shanghai?" she suddenly snapped.

I shrugged. "I disguised myself as a boy. Hired on ships as a sailor. Lied, cheated, misrepresented myself. Until I got here."

A sly smile lit her face. "Now, that finally sounds like a Pan." Her eyes bored into mine. I quickly averted my gaze from her, fearing she would hypnotize me.

"But how did you hear of–us? Of the remaining Pan family?" her son demanded, his voice harsh and threatening.

I edged toward the window. "When I arrived here in Shanghai, I hired an old tutor, to teach me your dialect. He noticed my ring. He told me the well-known tale of the great ancestor Pan Fulong, the White Pan, who sailed away with the Ming Emperor's eunuch Zheng He, leaving his great trading empire in the hands of his cousin–a man whose cruelty had earned him the title of Black Pan."

"*To survive and prosper one must be cruel!*" she interrupted savagely. "Cruelty is merely what the vanquished call the victors."

I took another step closer to the window.

"My tutor also said," I continued, "that the Black Pans held the trading empire only until the White Pan–or a descendant–returned to claim it again for the White Pan."

"And you–*you* dare to proclaim yourself the fabled White Pan?" she hissed. "You—a mere girl! An uncultured, ignorant, *foreign* girl from a fantastic excuse of an island, called, called–what?"

"Cuba!" I fairly shouted back. "And I'm not here to steal your empire. I'm here to–to discuss my family's role in your empire. To–"

"Oh, we know what you're here for," she interrupted. "The ancient agreement is clear, regardless of what you say. The Blacks return all to the White once he–or she–appears to claim it. Really, it doesn't matter what you think about it."

She stared hard at me for several minutes. I tried hard not to tremble. Or to glance at the tempting window. "My son," she suddenly said. He bent to her. "Bring your younger brother here."

"But I do not know that he has risen yet, Honored Mother," he whispered.

The sun was well up in the sky outside.

"Then rouse him!" she hissed back. He left hurriedly.

We were alone in the room. She stared hard at me for another several minutes, seeming to appraise me. "Take a seat," she commanded. "You are what–sixteen years?"

"Fifteen," I answered as I sat on the couch, very conscious of my youthfulness.

More appraisal. "Healthy?" she asked.

I nodded, warily.

"Have you begun your cycles yet?"

"That is none of your business!" I spit back.

A dry laugh from her. "Oh, my young lady, that is very much my business. Because you are about to become my beloved daughter."

"What?" I said as I jumped up. *Help me, Ma Tsu. What had she said?*

"Oh yes," she nodded, calm in the face of my agitation. "Let us speak plainly, dear daughter." She picked up the ring from the desk. "This ring indeed appears genuine. The ring of the fabled, lost White Pan, the able but sickeningly virtuous Pan Fulong. How our ancestor hated him."

She jerked her head toward the man in the portrait. "The original Black Pan. Bad luck dogged him. Bad luck, while his sanctimonious cousin went from success to success, attracting the attention even of the Yong Le Emperor's chief eunuch. But the Black Pan finally got what he lusted for, when the White Pan sailed away, never to return."

She tossed the ring in the air, and caught it with surprising skill. "Until an uncultured waif suddenly appears three hundred years later, imagining–ha!–that we would simply hand over our empire–and our fortune–to her. Ha! No, we have worked much too hard to do that, my dear."

She leaned toward me. I shrank back.

"Here is what we are going to do, my dear. In a minute, my youngest son will walk through that door. He is a Black Pan. Not too intelligent. Fond of cruelty. Like the first one, in the painting." She smiled. For some reason, her smile frightened me, more than her baleful stare.

"But Black Pan males," she continued, "are surprisingly easy to manipulate, once you learn what they want. Really, it is us, the women, who have ruled the Black Pans all these centuries, my dear daughter. You see, I am being plain with you, my dear."

Her eyes gleamed. "You have a choice, my dear. You can become my daughter-in-law. I will instruct you how to be a woman, my child. It is difficult, transforming from a girl into a woman. *Agonizing, in some ways.* But we will manage it, you and I." Another cold smile. Her tongue flicked out from between vermilion lips.

"I… I do not know that I wish your instruction," I croaked, my throat tight.

A short laugh from her. "Oh, you do have a choice, my dear. You can marry my youngest son, and join the White Pans and the Black Pans into a new, united Pan family."

"Or?" I asked, guessing the answer.

Her smile broadened, then suddenly disappeared, as she spat out her answer.

"Or we will slit your throat, take the ring for ourselves, and pretend you never existed. It is all the same to us, whichever you choose. But choose you must."

My heart stopped for several beats. This seemed the time for me to leave. I was about to dash for the window when the door opened.

The older son entered first, behind him a young man, about my age, strikingly handsome, actually, in a dissolute sort of way. He glanced at me from sleepy eyes.

"Honored Mother," he said, bowing casually before her.

She sighed, indulgently. "My youngest son. Meet your betrothed. The long-awaited White Pan, returning from some obscure island with a very difficult name, in the eastern ocean." She handed the ring to the boy. "Is she not beautiful?"

He turned to me, and looked me up and down absently. He said nothing as he slipped the ring onto his little finger. The ring he gave a most detailed examination.

"Oldest son, help me up," the woman said. "Get to know each other," she said to her youngest as she took his brother's arm and left the room. "You two are made for each other. It is in the stars."

The door shut. The boy yawned, and slouched toward the couch. I edged away from it. He flopped himself down on the silk covering. "Come," he said imperiously.

I didn't move, but glanced toward the window.

He undid his sash and opened his gown. "Come," he repeated, loudly this time.

I moved away, and looked for the latch on the window. Faster than I could have credited him, he sprang up and grabbed my arm in one hand. In his other a knife had appeared. I stared at it in horror. The gleaming blade was very long, its edge very sharp. The gilded handle was studded with rubies and pearls.

With slow deliberation he brought the knife to my throat. "You heard what my dear mother said. We must get to know each other," he said with a broad smile. "It won't take long. Perhaps you'll even enjoy it," he added, pulling me to the couch.

I began to struggle, trying to wrench free of his grip. He laughed, and hit me in the face with the handle of the knife. I felt the rubies rip into my skin, and tasted blood.

"Next time, it will be the blade, not the handle," he said with a snarl. He shoved me onto the couch on my back, and moved over me.

He put the hand with the knife on the couch beside me, to support himself as he pinned me down with his other hand on my shoulder. As he lowered himself toward me, with the knife no longer at my throat, I shoved with both hands against his chest as hard as I could. The shove sent him spinning away. He lost his footing, and fell flat on his face on the carpet with a surprised little cry.

Silence. Breathing hard, I sprang off the couch, and glanced at him on the carpet.

He was still. Unnaturally still. And beneath him, spreading out through the cream carpet, was a pool of red. The red reached the phoenix in the center of the carpet.

I took a few hesitant steps to the body, praying to *Ma Tsu* all the way, grabbed a shoulder, and turned him over.

Yes. His knife handle was sticking out of his chest. The blade was all the way in. He had fallen on it. I remembered what his evil mother had said, about Black Pan males being dogged by bad luck.

I grabbed his hand, and twisted the ring off his limp finger. I put the ring back on my finger–where it belonged. *Thank you, Ma Tsu, for helping me reclaim my ring.*

This seemed a good time to use that garden window and take my farewell of the Black Pans and their happy, though now smaller, family. As I slipped outside, I wondered how long I had before they came after me. Now I really did need *Ma Tsu's* help, all she had to offer. I began to run as soon as I was outside.

* * * * *

I reached my room just beyond the eastern city wall in no time. When I burst through the door, my tutor was there. Tall, thin, in a threadbare grey gown, the kindly old man had adopted me soon after my arrival in Shanghai. He had taught me the dialect, and many things about China–including the Black Pans and White Pans.

"You are alive!" he said, genuinely surprised to see me.

"Yes. The Black Pans are as charming a family as you said they would be," I said, quickly stuffing my few clothes and things into a bag, including the purse of gold I had reserved for my return to Cuba.

"In a hurry?" he asked as he watched me.

"Yes, a bit of a hurry. I left the younger son dead in the library. I'm afraid I ruined their expensive carpet there." I headed for the door.

"You killed the Black Pans younger son?" he asked in astonishment.

"No! He tried to force himself on me, we struggled, and he fell on his own knife, the clumsy idiot."

The old man's face was aghast. "You murdered a Black Pan!"

"Not *murdered*," I repeated. "He slipped and killed himself. But I strongly suspect his mother won't appreciate the distinction. Nor the giant Tanka doorman."

"You'd better run," he snapped at me. "Right now, and the farther the better."

"That had occurred to me, also. Thank you for all your help, old man."

He bowed, and reached into the capacious sleeve of his thin gown. "Take this. I thought that, if you survived and I saw you again, it would be useful to you." He crossed the room to the door, where I was standing impatiently, and put a beautiful green and red cloisonne disc in my hand, an ivory ring in its center, silver chains on either side.

"That's very lovely, old one. Thank you," I said hurriedly, and turned.

"Wait. It is more than lovely. Watch." So saying, he depressed the ivory ring in the center. A faint whirring sound, and a thin ring of metal bloomed around the outside edge of the disc, as the chains fell off. The metal ring was razor sharp.

"It is a throwing star," he explained. "Exquisitely balanced. Deadly. Practice it on the ship." He depressed the ivory again, and the blades retracted. He inserted the chains in their hooks again, and placed the disc around my neck.

"The Black Pans will find you," he said, urgently, staring me full in my face, his hands on my shoulders. "Wherever you go, they will find you. You must be prepared. The throwing star will help. Good luck. Hurry. Try the Kaikan wharf, second from the north in Nan Tao–barbarian ships are often leaving from there."

I hugged him, much to his discomfort, turned, and fled. Out to the alley, and down to the Whampoa River, the north end of the docks. As I ran onto the Kaikan wharf, I saw a Dutch bilander just pulling away from the dock. My legs were nearly numb from all the running, but even so I stumbled to the edge of the dock, and jumped. I barely made it across the growing space to the moving ship, landing with a thud against cotton bales, and scrambled onto the deck with my bag in front of an amazed Dutch sailor.

"Where are you going?" I asked in Spanish, out of breath. He stared dumbly.

I tried English, which I spoke better than Dutch. "What is your destination?"

His face lit up. "Canton, first," he answered.

"That will do." Ships left Canton for Manila frequently. I'd catch a Spanish galleon there for Veracruz, then cross Mexico and a final short sea voyage to Cuba. I glanced back at the docks as we sailed slowly up the Whampoa River with our cargo of cotton and Shanghai's newest criminal. No sign of the Black Pans. But as my tutor had said–they would follow. All the way to Havana, I suspected.

Chapter Two. Jim Hawkins. West Devon Coast, England, Spring 1756

The bar silver and the arms still lie, for all that I know, where Captain Flint buried them; and certainly they shall lie there for me. Oxen and wain-ropes would not bring me back again to that accursed island. –Ch. 34, Treasure Island, *Robert Louis Stevenson*

Our sign swung wildly in the spring storm's heavy wind. The notch in the wood where Billy Bones' sword had missed Black Dog gleamed in the occasional flash of lightning, below the words "Admiral Benbow Inn."

Billy Bones. The old pirate with the saber cut across his cheek, who drew Long John Silver's pirate shipmates to our quiet inn on the West Devon coast last year, searching for the treasure map Bones carried in his sea chest. How much had changed since then, I thought, staring at the rain pelting down outside the parlour window. My mother had decamped for London with the good Dr. Livesey as her new husband shortly after my return from Treasure Island. Being the custodian of my new wealth until I am twenty-one, mother left me to manage the lonely inn above the cove.

The nightmare had begun soon after mother had left. I'd awake, drenched in sweat, just after Blind Pew thrust the black spot in Billy Bones' hand. And then I'd hear it, distinctly, downstairs. The peculiar thudding noise made by Billy Bones' dead body as it hit our parlour floor, the rum and imminent arrival of Silver's pirates too much for his black old heart.

Soon, I came to look forward to the sound every night. The haunting thud came to stand for my escape from the dull routine of the inn. From listening to Devon country folks' small stories of small happenings in small lives. Billy Bones' hitting the floor took me away from all this, to the delicious feel of a ship jumping as the sails caught a fresh breeze, to the explosion of my pistol blasting Israel Hands from the port shrouds of the *Hispaniola* as I sat pinned to the mast by his knife.

But tonight–tonight I was here, alone, trapped not a yard from where Billy Bones had hit the floor. Restless, hating the storm and the cold and indeed the old inn itself, I glared out the parlour window at the dark pathway down to the cove, waiting for the next flash of lighting.

Wait! What was that? Shivers swept me as a figure materialized on the pathway in the lightning's sudden glare–then just as suddenly disappeared into the darkness. A one-legged man, struggling against the wind and rain, the familiar crutch under the left arm.

Long John Silver? At the Admiral Benbow? I fell away from the window, gasping for breath, as if struck in the stomach. I rushed to the plank door and jammed the iron bolt across it. Turning, I stumbled to the bar, and jerked the pistol from under the rough oak counter. Checked the powder, and stuck it under my vest with a trembling hand.

Seconds ago I was pining for the adventures of last year. Now that they seemed to return, I was trembling with fear. But perhaps I was mistaken. Could I believe my eyes?

Two huge blows on the door shook the glasses on the counter. He wasn't an apparition. Open the door and serve the devil a glass of rum? Or do as my mother and I had done just over a year ago, and flee out the back to hide under the bridge?

To my credit, I believe, I walked to the door, threw open the bolt, and opened it.

There he stood, the grizzled old buccaneer himself, looming above me in the storm. Water streamed off Long John Silver's greatcoat, his tricorner hat barely protecting his large, crafty face from the pelting rain. Even in the storm, he swept off the hat grandly, smiled broadly at me–too broadly–and bowed.

"By the powers, my boy, ye look good. Have ye a glass of rum for an old shipmate, lad, whilst we parley over a scheme of mine?"

My feelings for Long John Silver were by no means as warm as the apparent smile he was presenting me. I motioned him to enter with a jerk of my head.

"Ah, thankee, Jim Hawkins. You always was a kind boy, to my thinking," said he, hobbling into the parlour. He threw his drenched greatcoat and tricorner hat over a chair beside the fire, before which he leaned on his crutch, rubbing his hands together.

"The old claws get numb from cold much faster these days, my lad," he announced cheerfully over his shoulder to me.

I passed to the bar, poured our cheapest rum into a glass, and silently crossed to him and set it on a nearby table. I noted that though his hair had more gray, his clothes were fine. Indeed, though it seemed strange on him, he had all the marks of a prosperous gentleman. Linen shirt, clean yet; woolen britches; and a silk vest. His hair even appeared to have been subjected to a comb but recently.

His quick eyes took in my look. He was always a clever one. "Yes, by thunder! I be quite the gentleman now, do I not?" He took the glass in hand, and raised it in a toast.

"To old times, eh? Even those times, sadly enough, that be filled with sorrow and misunderstandings. But shared, all the same, says I."

He took a deep drink of the rum, and stood there, savoring the warmth apparently.

"Why are you here?" I asked coldly.

An insincere laugh from Long John, and a sideways glance at me. "Quick to business, my boy. You always was quick to business."

Silence from me. He was too dangerous a person to be easy or familiar with.

"You're right, of course," he continued. "Smart as paint, you are. I seed it from the first time I laid eyes on you, in me old tavern in Bristol." He emptied his rum.

"Here be the long and short of it, my boy. As you can see from my garb, I've not done badly since I last had the pleasure of seeing you on Treasure Island. My old missus met me in Havana, with all me savings from Cap'n England and Cap'n Flint, plus the sale of me tavern in Bristol. A tidy sum, it were. I'm a prosperous tobaccy grower in a valley southwest of Havana, my boy."

"Then why are you here?" I repeated.

He studied the empty glass on the table. I was not going to offer him more rum.

"That be a ripe question, my boy. And here be the unvarnished truth. I miss it, lad. All of it. The feel of wind filling the sail and pushing you forward. Being on a ship, going–anywhere. There's no feeling like it, says I. No roadway nor path nor sign hemming you in. But the best, says I, is when you're going after *treasure*. And you and I knows where there's more treasure, don't we, Jim Hawkins?"

His face glowed in the firelight as he spoke, and his eyes began to twitch. He glanced over at me, just like the old days, his face flushed with the longing for treasure. Despite myself, my heart was beating fast, such was the magic he could conjure up.

But this was Long John Silver, I remembered. A man who had killed, lied, and betrayed to get his prosperous tobacco plantation in Cuba. I hid my excitement. "What treasure would that be, Long John?" I asked, even though I knew the answer.

"Why, Flint's silver bars, still on Treasure Island!" he exclaimed. "Look on your map, boy. Remember the other two X's on that chart? Up by the North Inlet? 'Arms be here,' by one X. And 'Silver bars be here,' by t' other. Arms I ain't interested in. But silver bars? That'd be a treasure worth huntin' for, boy!"

"Then go hunt it," said I.

"Aye, easy to say. But it's a big island. And tho' I had your treasure map in me claws once, my attention was focus'd on the other hoard, the one Ben Gunn beat us to. I didn't rightly pay attention to the silver bars. Certainly not enough to find it on me own."

"So you're here to talk me out of the map, then," I concluded. "In that you're flat out of luck, Long John."

A trace of anger swept over his large face, quickly displaced by a wily curiosity.

"And where might it be, boy? With your mother?"

I laughed. "My mother's living in London now. With our friend Dr. Livesey."

More astonishment on Long John's face, then he burst into laughter, and indeed spent the better part of a minute with his whole body shaking, slapping his thighs, and laughter pealing from his mouth. He very nearly fell off the chair.

"Why, by thunder, if that ain't the way of the world," he finally gasped. "She's took your treasure, and she's spending it with the good doctor in London!"

Another fit of laughter shook the parlour. I sat, sour and silent.

"My boy, you need them silver bars now worse than me, says I. You've more reason to return to Treasure Island than your old shipmate, and you may lay to that!"

"Nay," I said. "There'll still be plenty of my own treasure left for me, when I reach my majority."

"You're what–fifteen now? Sixteen?"

"Fifteen."

"Jim, my boy, you'd be surprised how much a woman can spend in six years. Or a man, for that matter. I wouldn't have believed how much Blind Pew spent in one year. He was a rich man after Flint's last voyage, and in a year he was swindlin' and knifin' for a piece of bread."

"I don't need the money," I persisted.

Silver glanced sideways at me again, that shrewd glance of his I knew so well.

"P'haps. But what about t' other, me lad? The adventure. The freedom of going wherever ya please over the wide blue of the sea? Do ya nae think of that, me lad?"

"Never," I lied. My heart was racing again, despite my words.

He grunted. "Bad storm today, Jim. Do ya ever bring to mind the warm days and balmy evenings of the Caribbean, my boy? Going about yore business with naught but a shirt and britches, not even shoes much of the time? Do ya a mind of that, Jim?"

"Not a bit," I lied again. "I have summers here, in England."

"Aye," he said softly. "All *two weeks* of summer, here in England. And the rest of the year–this." He hobbled to the window, and stared out at the stormy darkness.

I couldn't help myself. "Besides, how would we even get back to Treasure Island?" I heard myself asking, trying to sound casual-like.

He stood very still at the window. He thought he had me. "Ah, yes. Smart as paint," he said softly. He turned on his crutch, trying hard to conceal the triumph from his face. "As I told ye, I'm a prosperous tobaccy grower in Cuba. Got me own ship, I do. By the powers, she's a beauty. She's down in your cove right now, with my crew, Jim."

He smiled. His clothes might be grand, but his teeth were the same chipped, yellow fangs as always.

"We could sail tonight, my boy. I've learned a lot since Treasure Island. I can set my own course, now. Latytude, even longytude, after a fashion. Shall we sail, Jim?"

The question hung in the parlour, as the fire crackled. The notion drew me, pulled me towards it, as a flame pulls a moth. With a jolt, I shook my head. "I don't have the map, Long John," I blurted out. "It's at the Squire's mansion."

"By thunder! What's it doing there?" he roared, anger lighting his face.

My guard up again, I took my time to answer, throwing another log on the fire. "I've been spending time there. You've learned to calculate latitude, longitude–well, so have I. Plus even more mathematics. And geography. He's teaching me the fine life."

"And very large of him it is, I'm sure. And he's relieved you of the map, has he?"

"Well, he likes to show it to his friends when they visit."

The fire crackled in the silence. “My lad, I’ve come a might long ways for that map, by the powers,” Long John said quietly, an ominous undertone in his voice. “Let’s us just visit the Squire, get the map, and you and me go treasure-huntin’, eh?”

“Oh, no. He wouldn’t appreciate seeing you, Long John. He’s likely in fact to throw you behind bars. Walk me to the gate of The Hall, and I’ll talk with him. Alone.”

With a growl, he limped to the chair beside the fire and claimed his greatcoat and tricorner.

“Then we’d best be off, lad. I have my first mate with me. A fine boy, former slave that I freed. You’ll enjoy his company through the storm.”

* * * * *

For once, Long John had spoken truly. His first mate, Isaiah, was tall and strong, with white teeth that shined out of his black face even in the midst of a spring English storm. As we strode through the rain, he regaled us with tales of working the tobacco plantations on Cuba. We arrived at the gates to The Hall, which gleamed with candlelight at the end of the long avenue from the road.

“I won’t be long,” I promised. “Shelter under this oak ’till I return.” I dashed down the avenue, noticing several well-appointed carriages parked out front.

In a thrice the Squire’s butler had admitted me. As he led me to the den at the front of the great house, we passed the large library, where I saw the Squire and several ladies seated before a string quartet. Amongst them was a girl looking quite sour, playing with her long golden curls

Once in the den, I headed straight for the oak desk beside a half-open window. There, displayed prominently, was the map of Treasure Island. How often I had seen the Squire pick it up with a flourish and present it to a visitor, carrying on about murders and pitched battles quite beyond those that actually occurred. Staring at the old parchment, my hatred of the island came back to me. Was I actually considering returning there?

Soon the Squire’s considerable bulk bustled into the room, bedecked in linen and silk and powdered wig. "Jim, Jim! What a pleasant surprise. And the timing could not be better, upon my word! One of my guests has a young daughter just your age with her. Perhaps a trifle older, two years. Four, mayhaps. But she has her eye on you! And a better match you couldn't imagine. Why, she's positively rolling in money. She–"

"Squire Trelawney, sir, that's wonderful. But, uh, I've had a proposal that I need your counsel on. To go adventuring again–to the Caribbean, in fact."

"What? Errant nonsense, boy. You've had your adventure. Time to settle down and enjoy your fortune, eh?" He clapped his pudgy arm on my shoulder. "Marry a rich heiress, what? Fox hunts on the weekend and all. Soon enough there'll be children dashing about underfoot!" This last with an exaggerated wink of his eye.

"But...I don't know if I'm ready for all that."

"Posh. Another year or two managing the inn, maybe three or four, then it's the life of the gentry for you, boy! Be patient. Let me introduce you to the young lady. Wait here, and I'll come for you after the piece has ended!"

My mind raced as he returned to the library. A girl? Four years older, yet? Years more at the Admiral Benbow? Then fox hunts and children underfoot?

My eyes strayed to the treasure map. I stepped up to the desk, and saw the red X marking the location of the silver bars, just west of the North Inlet. Some raindrops were blowing in the open window, and I put my hand on the latch to pull it shut.

What was that? Voices floated in from outside. Long John and Isaiah singing at the gate, their voices coming in pieces through the storm.

Fifteen men on the dead man's chest,
Drink and the devil had done for the rest!
Yo ho ho and a bottle of rum!
But one man of her crew alive,
What put to sea with seventy five!
Yo ho ho and a bottle of rum!

The old wicked song betrayed me. In the darkness outside the window, I saw pirates, was caressed by the flower-scented breeze of a Caribbean evening, smelled the salt of the sea, felt the lurch of the ship under my bare feet as the wind filled the sails.

Behind me, I heard the string quartet from the library, saw the girl waiting for me there, fidgeting with her curls, felt the weight of tending to the Admiral Benbow, wiping up spilled beer and sour vomit. Before I knew it, my wicked hand had snatched the map from the desk, and I had squeezed through the window opening and dropped to the ground. My wicked feet scarce touched dirt before I was running up the avenue, stuffing the treasure map under my shirt, yelling at Long John and Isaiah to move with haste.

The one-legged man could hobble with surprising speed. He hardly slowed Isaiah and me, and soon the dark bulk of the Admiral Benbow loomed before us. I didn't rightly expect the Squire to chase after us, with his elegant guests at The Hall, but the good gentleman was greatly fond of the map now in my shirt.

I had just scribbled a note to my mother when Long John stumbled to the door.

"Have ye Billy Bones' sea chest still, my lad?" he wheezed, face flushed.

I looked up. "Why, yes. In my room. Should we take it?"

"I would advise it," he gasped. "Mainly for the sent'mental airs of his old shipmate–but who knows what might still be in that chest of value to us, says I."

I was too rushed to dispute with him, and after throwing water on the fire, I dashed upstairs to my room. I was dragging the chest from the corner when Long John entered. He gazed in surprise at the maps crowding every inch of wallspace.

"Ye're a regular chart room, you are, my boy."

"I know every mile of coast in the Caribbean," I claimed, rather too proudly.

The old buccaneer's shrewd eyes were taking in the room. "And there be a very modern sextant, to boot. Bring it with us, my lad. It tops my old double quadrant, for fig'ring latytude, you may lay to that. Isaiah, fetch that sea chest of my old friend Billy Bones, if ye'd please."

I gathered the sextant as Isaiah entered and hefted the heavy chest handily.

"Why, shiver me timbers! Be that one of them new chronometers, for estimatin' longytude?" Long John's eyes were bulging at the precision timepiece on my table.

"Dr. Livesey brought that to me from London," said I, with unseemly pride again.

"And he is quite the trump for doing so, as the Squire might say," Long John answered. "Might I persuade you to bring that along also, my boy?"

I grabbed the chronometer. "We'd best be off, Long John. I don't expect the Squire to pursue us, but–"

"Aye, lad. Brisk to business you always was, and right ye be. Let's off!"

We emerged into the unabated storm. I locked the great door, put the key where my mother would know to find it, and turned to the cove with nary a backward glance.

"Step ahead, lads. Don't wait for your one-legged companion," Long John yelled above the wind, as he drew two double-barreled pistols from the pocket of his greatcoat.

"I'll brook no injury to the Squire or any of his men," I shouted back at him.

Long John saluted me, touching his forelock with his knuckles. "As ye order, Master Hawkins! I'll but announce courteous-like that we be dead bound to set sail."

It was amazing how easily Isaiah carried the huge sea chest down the steep, slippery path to the cove. Two longboats awaited us at the water's edge. "Captain Silver's coming soon," Isaiah shouted to the man in the near boat. "We'll go ahead and prepare to sail." He unloaded the chest into the second boat and he and I clambered into it, the sea on our legs feeling warmer than the chill air battering us. We each locked an oar, and within minutes had reached the smart little schooner offshore.

The sharp report of two pistol shots rang out behind us. I jerked my head back in time to see the orange flashes of two more shots, then darkness shrouded the cliff. Soon enough Long John's shape came hurtling out of the dark to the shore and the boat there.

Isaiah was shouting orders from bow to stern, and seamen were swarming up the riggings. Sails blossomed from every mast as Long John's skiff came alongside.

"Under way, lads!" Long John bawled out as half a dozen willing hands pulled him aboard the schooner. "Young Hawkins here has Flint's map in his shirt, and wants us to help him load silver bars onto our ship!"

Chapter Three. Tabitha. Havana, Cuba, Spring 1756

Momma's screams echo down the colonnade. I tear around the corner from the kitchens. The two big Bantu slaves are dragging Momma away from Mistress Ravenia's rooms. Beyond the open door the Commandante looks coldly on, his black ringbeard gleaming in the morning light.

One of the Bantus knocks me to the marble floor as I throw myself on them. They kick me down the hall as they drag Momma to the locked room beneath the staircase.

Momma, me, and the two Bantus are panting and covered in sweat by the time they throw us into the dark room and slam the door shut. We hear the clank of the lock.

"Momma, Momma. What's happening?"

She's moaning, breathing heavily, and covers her face with her hands.

"Momma? Tell me."

"She's sending–" she gasps for breath, her thin chest heaving. "Sending me away. To work the fields."

My breath catches in my throat. The plantations are death for slaves. From overwork, or disease, or beatings. But death, for sure.

"But–why?" I spit out.

She shakes her head, and begins wailing.

"Momma–why?" I grab her shoulders, and shake her.

Deep breathes, to pull herself together. "It's that cursed Commandante, Ravenia's latest lover. I seen how he looks at me. Hate and desire, together. He can't stand me near."

"But, the Mistress. You're her personal servant. She'll–"

A bitter laugh. "She's more a slave than you and me, Tabitha. Slave to him. He'll enjoy everything she has to give, then leave her. Just like all the others have."

"But Momma, Momma–"

"No! Listen. Tabitha." I feel her face close to mine in the darkness.

"Tabitha. I won't let you go with me to the fields."

"But–"

"No!" she shrieks. "You are all I have left of your father, child. You will not go."

She pants, and runs her fingers through her hair. Like she always does when she's scheming.

"When they come for me, I'll fight. Punch, scream, run, spit. Fight like an *orisha* from the darkest hell."

She begins to wail again, then catches herself.

"While they're battling me, you run, Tabitha. Run through the kitchen and into the alley. Run like *Chango* the thunder god is after you. Don't you stop for nothing, Tabitha. You understand me, daughter?"

I'm crying. *I'm gonna lose my momma.*

"Understand?" she shrieks, grabbing my shoulders.

"But Momma–where am I running to?" I gasp, as sobs begin to shake me.

"The street, child. You live on the street. Under the bridges. In the alleys. There's other runaway slaves out there."

"But Momma, I don't know how to–"

"Then you learn how to, girl. And fast."

"But Momma–"

"Tabitha!" She jerks the white amulet from her neck, and shoves it in my hand. "This is yours now, girl. Remember all the times I told you how your father gave it to me, just before they beat him to death on the slave ship? A piece of *Obatala* is in it, Tabitha. This is a dark world, but *Obatala* keeps us Yoruba people pure, clean. The amulet has kept me alive, to raise you in your father's memory. Now it will keep you alive. It is yours."

Her hands twitch as she ties its leather strands around my neck.

"Now hold me, Tabitha. Hold your momma close. We won't have much time together, my dear daughter."

We weep, and hold each other close in the dark of the closet.

They are back, soon, much sooner than we wish. Momma shoves me away from her as the key clanks in the lock. She launches herself out and upon them as the light pierces our darkness. Whirling, shouting, kicking, cursing. I catch a glimpse of the Bantu's arms fending off her struggles, and beyond that the Commandante on the veranda, looking on in alarm.

I dash out, and veer right, toward the kitchens, my legs pumping fast, like my momma told me. I hear the Commandante shout behind me.

"The girl! I want her, too!"

Nearly to the kitchen corner, I glance back. Momma has broken free of the Bantus, and is running up the veranda, toward the Commandante–away from me, I realize, luring them all away from me. She glances back to check my progress.

A metallic twang fills the veranda, as the Commandante draws his sword, the short one he carries everywhere with him. He jabs it into Momma–*my momma*!–as she runs by him. Her body stiffens, jerks to a halt.

I shriek, again and again. The veranda tilts, and spins, and jerks.

Momma turns her head to me, her eyes wide with surprise. Her eyes are the only thing in the world that isn't spinning. She tries to say something. Can't. Then her mouth makes the shape of the word she can't say.

Run.

I can't move. Momma's body slumps. The Commandante yells to the Bantus.

"Get the girl!"

My momma's gone.

Hands pull me from behind. The kitchen women, Yoruba like us. They whirl me around, and shove me into the kitchen.

"Run, Tabitha! Obey your momma."

I stumble toward the back door. I am running fast now, like my momma told me. I glance back. The women are shoving carts into the kitchen aisle, to slow the Commandante. I run faster, and burst through the door and into the street.

My momma's gone.

* * * * *

Hidden behind barrels in the alley east of the square, my friend Xavier and I watch the Commandante stride into the Plaza de Armas. For such a big man, the Commandante always moves quickly, although jerkily, as though he is avoiding something.

It is the ghosts of all those he has killed, I suddenly understand. They clamor about him, whispering sly comments, promising their revenge.

My momma is there, in the crowd of spirits. And I will have that revenge. I feel the heavy weight of the pistol in my belt. It was not difficult to steal the pistol. The Spanish are so careless. So sloppy. Weapons are left about everywhere. This one was on the table just inside the guardhouse at the south gate of the la Fuerza Castle, looming on the far end of the square. It only has one bullet in it, but that is all I will need.

I've thought about it often, in these two weeks on the streets as a runaway. It'll be late in the morning, in the barbershop off Avenida Aguiar, when the Commandante is stretched out on the big leather chair, the thin barber trimming his ringbeard. His eyes will be shut, and the barber will be concentrating on the trim. I have it all planned out. Xavier will walk in and distract the barber. Then I'll quietly slip in, up to the chair, and put the pistol on the side of his head, just above the ear. I've decided not to say anything, about momma. That might give him or the barber time to do something. I'll just walk up, both hands holding the heavy pistol, put the barrel against his head, and pull the trigger.

And then run. Again. Just like momma told me.

I met Xavier my first day on the streets. He is Yoruba, like me, though younger by a year or two. Twelve, or thirteen. But he's lived on the street for over a year. He says the amulet of *Obatala* that momma gave me is powerful good luck. That it will permit me to kill the Commandante. And get away.

He taught me how to steal things from the Spanish. How to sleep during the day and live during the night, when the darkness hides us, and the Spanish are busy with the women and the gambling and the rum. Where to go to get food from the slaves in the markets and the kitchens of the big mansions.

Xavier taught me where to sleep, behind the barrels littering the alleys. You can depend on the Spanish to leave things around, to be sloppy and unorganized. We marvel, Xavier and me, how the Spanish can rule over us, being so careless. We have decided it is because they are so large. And they have large things, like horses. And hard things, like guns. The steel and the horses and their large bodies make up for their sloppiness and inability to do anything right.

But still it is a puzzle, how they manage to rule us.

He is even thinner than I am, Xavier. Big eyes, same jet black skin. But he smiles much more than I do. What do I have to smile about? My momma is gone, to the realm of the *orisha*. My daddy gone, during the voyage from Africa. All I have is the amulet of *Obatala*. And my revenge on the Commandante.

"Tomorrow morning, Xavier," I whisper to him as we watch the Commandante in the Plaza.

Xavier grins. He nods his head. "That barber–boy, is he gonna be mad at losing such a good customer," he laughs.

"Maybe we'll let you take the Commandante's slot," I suggest. "Won't be long 'till you're needin' a shave."

We both laugh at that. Xavier, though younger, has taught me a lot. Including how to laugh. After I kill the Commandante, I expect I'll laugh a lot. If I'm alive.

Xavier slumps back against the barrels at the front of the alley. We've been eating scrap pieces of *tasaro*, turtle meat, from the bottom of the barrels for two days now.

"That *tasaro's* too salty. I need me some wine."

I snort. "It'll go to your head, Xavier. Besides, where you gonna get wine?"

"From that guardhouse," he proclaims in the braggin' sort of way he has. He points to the Castle's guardhouse across the Plaza, the same one I stole my pistol from.

"Watch me," he says, and rises.

Before I can stop him, he's slipped away, and making his way around the edge of the square. Though skinny, he's awfully strong, and moves quick and smooth. I follow him with my eyes. He's a friend, but he does things too quickly, without thinking them through, to my mind. Impulsive.

The Commandante is walking through the square still, jerky as always, with his fat lieutenant waddling after him. I see that the Commandante is heading for the guardhouse also. Does Xavier notice that? I begin to worry. I've seen Xavier slip out of some bad situations. But he doesn't have a lucky amulet, like I have.

Xavier slips around the corner and into the guardhouse. The Commandante approaches the guardhouse in his jerky walk. I begin to moan, nervous.

A moment later, there's a yell, and Xavier comes barreling out, a bottle of wine in his hand, a triumphant smile on his face.

He runs smack into the Commandante, who grabs him by the neck. Xavier swings the bottle at him, but the Commandante knocks it out of his hands.

Xavier is struggling, trying to hit the Commandante, who draws his short sword, with the metallic twang I heard two weeks ago.

No. Not with the same sword that took my momma. Please, no. I tug the pistol from my belt, and grip it with both hands. Lifting it up, I sight down the shaking steel barrel. Much too far. I would be lucky to hit the guardhouse, much less the Commandante. Do I run into the Plaza to get closer? No. The fat lieutenant would stop me long before I got to the Commandante's side.

I begin to sob, for Xavier.

The Commandate hits Xavier on the head with the butt of the sword, the big hand guard on its end. Xavier slumps, stunned.

"Ha!" the Commandante laughs, triumph in his high voice, as he throws Xavier's limp body into the dust. "Another runaway slave. My morning is complete."

The fat lieutenant, Sanchez, guffaws loudly. It is smart for him to agree with everything the Commandante says.

"The third, I believe, this week, Sanchez?" He bends down, takes Xavier's neck in one large hand, and quickly draws his sword across a cheek, three quick slices. Even from the other side of the Plaza, I can see the blood on the sword.

"Put him in the cage, Lieutenant," says the Commandante, nodding toward the steel cage hanging from the Ceiba silk-cotton tree on the east edge of the Plaza, not fifty feet on my right. "We'll see how long the ruffian lasts." More laughs, then a sigh of contentment, at how well the morning is going. He wipes the sword on Xavier's pants, then returns it to its scabbard, and stands enjoying the morning, hand patting the butt of the sword.

The lieutenant picks up Xavier easily, and drags him through the dust to the cage. Another soldier, from the guardhouse, unlocks the door to the cage, and shakes out the bones of the last person to be placed there, some weeks earlier.

The cage is a hard way to die. The person in it exhausts himself–or herself–fighting off the hungry flies and birds that torture them as they starve and lose their strength. In the end they are eaten alive by the flies and birds.

I watch with horror as Xavier is dumped into the cage, the door is locked, and the cage is raised off the ground by the rope over the Ceiba tree's lowest branch.

Xavier comes to, rises to his knees, and his scream echoes around the Plaza as he realizes where he is. And what will happen to him in the next days.

I crouch behind the barrel in the alley, listening to Xavier's screams, which turn to low moans as the day ends. Several times soldiers visit the cage, and amuse themselves by poking Xavier with their swords, and commenting on the flies already massing on his bloody cheek. Xavier still has strength to fight off the birds which flutter hungrily around the cage.

By nightfall, I know what I must do for my friend.

Taking care, I very slowly make my way along the edge of the square under the night's cover. I will not be caught, not before my revenge on the Commandante, at least.

I will miss the pistol. But I will find another one, for the Commandante. But carefully. Not impulsively, like Xavier. That was his problem, his impulsive way. Never will I be impulsive.

I check the guardhouse. Nothing but the light of a candle, and the occasional laughter of the guards.

I am beside the tree. All around it are offerings, to the *orisha* which dwells in the tree. Candles, and plates of fruit, yellow bananas and red *mamey colorado,* gleaming in the faint candlelight. The tree is much visited by slaves and freed people, those of us who realize its age and size are signs of the presence of an *orisha*.

Strange, how the Spanish can be so clever at some things, but so blind to the *orisha*.

"Xavier," I whisper urgently as I arrive beside the cage.

A moan from the heap at the bottom of the cage.

"Xavier!"

A head rises. "Tabitha?"

"I'm sorry," I begin. Then my throat tightens up, and I cannot speak.

"Tabitha. I'm just sorry I won't see you kill the Commandante," he says, in a cracked voice.

He and I don't need words, so I forget them.

"Here." I shove the pistol, with its one bullet, through the bars of the cage.

"What?" he asks.

"For you. Before the flies and the birds have their way."

A sharp breath, as he realizes the gift I am giving him.

"But the Commandante–"

"Plenty of pistols to be stolen," I say. "You know how sloppy the Spanish are."

A weak laugh. Even now, Xavier laughs.

"Thanks."

I nod. "Don't delay. You will need strength to do it."

"Thanks."

I move away in the darkness.

I am slumped behind the *tasaro* barrels in the alley when the shot shatters the silence of the night.

Chapter Four. Jim Revisits Treasure Island

The doctor opened the seals with great care, and there fell out the map of an island…above all, three crosses of red ink–two on the north part of the island, one in the south-west… Over on the back the same hand had written this further information: 'the bar silver is in the north cache; you can find it by the trend of the east hummock, ten fathoms south of the black crag with the face on it.' –Ch. 6, Treasure Island, *Robert Louis Stevenson*

A month later we approached the cursed island on which the infamous pirate Jack Flint had buried his ill-gotten treasure. As I clutched the riggings of the port shrouds to steady myself on the deck, we sailed past Spyglass Hill, where a year ago we discovered Ben Gunn had beat us to Flint's gold. The sharp clap of the wind in our sails reminded me suddenly of the explosion of Long John's double-barreled pistols as he had shot George Merry dead beside the empty chests on that hill.

This time, we were after Flint's silver. Soon we had turned the corner of the island, and rode the wind west past Rum Cove on the north coast, above which Ben Gunn's old cave was barely visible through the undergrowth. Well I remembered my weary four days in the back of that cave last year, bagging doubloons, ducats, moidores, double guineas, and pieces of eight from huge piles beside the more orderly quadrilaterals of stacked gold bars.

Ah well. My mother and Dr. Livesey were enjoying my share of Flint's gold in London, and in truth could not be more content than I, with my tanned skin and bare feet. I had not even worn my vest over my shirt for a month. The old sea smells of salt, tar, and rope were familiar in my nose by now. In my heart, I felt as free as the gulls which soared about the ship. The West Devon coast seemed very distant in every way, and glad I was of it. *The wind fills my heart as well as the sails. The salt in my blood calls to the salt of the sea, whose answer wraps me in an ancient embrace. I am at home, where I belong, at peace in the mystery of it all.*

Silver's ship, the *Pieces of Eight*, leaned into the wind pushing us towards Flint's silver. It was a trim schooner, perhaps big for the class, but very nicely lined. The decks and railings were a hardwood, mahogany by the look of it. Two square-rigged sails of the finest linen blossomed on the foremast, with a pair of large triangular jibs running up from the bowsprit jutting forward of the bow. The mizzenmast main sail was rigged fore-and-aft, with the two sails above it square. His crew seemed utterly devoted to the old buccaneer, as well they might, since all of them were, like the first mate Isaiah, former slaves freed by Silver. The only exception was Silver's quartermaster, an old mestizo half-Indian who everyone called Taino, after his Indian tribe.

Silver was on the poop deck, his hair wild in the wind, the old keen look of anticipation lighting his face. His fierce countenance reminded me of the look he'd had just before plunging his dirk into old Tom's back, as I watched hidden in the brush along the south beach of this island a year ago. Had he really changed much from then?

He suddenly cast a sharp look down at me, as if reading my thoughts. I forced a smile at him. "She runs well, Long John," I shouted to him over the wind.

"Aye, she slips through the water smooth," he agreed. "I've sheathed the bottom in copper, me lad. Keeps the damn teredo worms from me hull–plus it gives me two or three extra leagues every day," he claimed, laughing, his head thrown back.

So now I knew why the old pirate was so eager to return to Treasure Island for Flint's silver. He was using silver to pay for copper.

Some three miles past Rum Cover we sighted the mouth of the North

Inlet and beyond it the North Cape, on which the red X on my treasure map indicated the location of Flint's silver bars. Long John ordered Isaiah to bring in the sails, and we dropped anchor just where the inlet narrows.

"Master Hawkins, what says your treasure map about the silver bars?" Long John asked in a ringing voice from the poop deck, as Isaiah and the crew all crowded on the starboard railing, beyond which stretched rows of small hills, thick with vegetation.

I pulled the map from my shirt. On the back side of it, in the small, neat hand and same red ink of the X, I read. "The bar silver is in the north cache; you can find it by the trend of the east hummock, ten fathoms south of the black crag with the face on it."

"Aye, there you have it, lads," said Long John in the same ringing voice. "An extra share to the good man who first sights the black crag with the face on it amongst those hills." A great cheer arose from the men, and all scrambled to launch the long boat. Long John and I glanced at each other, and saw the same excitement in each other's face.

Treasure!

It was nearing sundown when Taino himself, the old quartermaster, began shouting that he'd found the face on the black crag. In a matter of moments we were all gathered about the rock. Indeed, something like a face was weathered into it, nose and mouth at least, especially when Taino had cut back the vines with his machete.

As one, our eyes turned south, and traveled the ground some ten fathoms to a low, hummocky hill that ran easterly. Isaiah bounded to the spot, and began tearing vines and chucking rocks from the side of the hill. Soon enough, an opening appeared, slanting downwards, barely large enough for a child. The crew crowded to the opening, but Isaiah barred all with his muscular arm. "This is for Cap'n Silver. And the lad," he announced.

Long John hobbled up, myself beside him. "You first, Jim," he grandly allowed. "The bulk of it'll be yours, and you be the proper size to fit into this here opening, says I."

As I passed him and squeezed in, he added, "And kindly keep a sharp eye out for snakes and spiders, me lad." The crew laughed, though I did not find it so humorous.

"Pass me that lantern," I requested curtly. Soon a lantern was lit and in my hand. I cautiously crept down the slope, hunched over, lantern in front. Nothing but cobwebs and roots for the first half dozen yards, then abruptly a series of steep downward steps, beyond which a large cavern opened up before me in the lantern's flickering light.

And, sure enough, right in the middle of the cavern, stacked neat as pins, half a dozen quadrilaterals of silver bars, each rising to a height of four feet or so.

And two skeletons, sprawled to either side of the silver.

I jumped once when I saw the silver, and again when I noticed the skeletons. With a shaking hand I held the lantern high, to ascertain what other surprises the cavern might hold. Roots hanging from the stony ceiling, some water dripping down the right wall, but nothing else.

"Hallo! Hallo down there!" Long John's voice echoed down the passageway.

A fancy took me, such as often takes my wicked mind. I grabbed a bar of silver off the closest stack, then gingerly gave a shake to the large forearm bone of the skeleton next to it. Thankfully, the bone disengaged easily. With my two gruesome trophies–for well I knew how many must have died to accumulate those six stacks of silver, beyond even the two skeletons still here–I pushed my way back up the passageway. I set down the lantern, crept to the opening, and hollered, "Lend me a hand!"

Several hands eagerly reached into the opening. Into one I thrust the bone, with a sudden yell as of pain and fright. The hands and the bone disappeared.

"Shiver me timbers! The boy's decomposed!" I heard Long John shriek.

A great uproar promptly ensued, with many a "By the powers!" and "By thunder!" and much worse. I let the curses and shrieks die down a bit, then tossed out the bar of silver. It hit the ground with a thud. A collective gasp went up, then stone silence.

I popped my head out. "Ain't there be any interest in the rest of the silver?" says I, all innocence.

Long John's eyes bulged at me for long moment, then he collapsed on the ground, clutching his sides and laughing till he well nigh choked himself. Soon most of the company was joining him, all except old Taino, who stood solemnly, shaking his head, thinking no doubt of the old days before the white people came and ruined his islands.

It took but several minutes to enlarge the opening, and soon all of us except Taino–to act as sentry, should the ceiling collapse or whatnot–were gathered about the silver, with our two lanterns illuminating the cavern. There were, of course, many "Hurrahs!" and more "By the powers!" and such, in spite of the presence of the skeletons. Presently Long John had organized a relay brigade, and set himself down on the floor of the cavern to count the bars as he handed them to the beginning of the line.

Whilst this pleasant duty was occurring, I took one of the lanterns and cautiously examined the far reaches of the cavern. The cave narrowed considerably at the back, and I was about to turn around and rejoin the rest when a reflection caught my eye. There, wedged into a shelf, were brass strips, holding what appeared to be a small chest. Gingerly I worked my hand to the side of the chest, and felt a handle. A sharp tug, and the chest moved a bit–along with a good deal of dirt, falling from the ceiling there. All heads jerked in my direction, and several men dove toward the opening of the cavern.

"It's a chest," I explained sheepishly to the wild eyes locked upon me.

Isaiah cautiously sidled over to me. "Nah, tain't a chest. Tis but a vanity box," he sneered. Cautiously he worked his hand on the other side, and gently slid the modest-sized chest out of its niche, carrying it over to where Silver sat.

Vanity box or chest, the container had a distinct style and composition to it.

"Lacquer! By thunder, I've never seen a chest of lacquer," Long John whispered, tilting its glinting surface in the lantern's shafts of light.

"And what in the world be those funny markings on it, Cap'n?" asked Isaiah.

Indeed, there were strange markings on the top of the chest, which put me of a mind of something I'd seen before, but couldn't rightly place. "Devil writing!" hissed one of the sailors in a quaking voice. Several lads began backing toward the entrance.

Long John gave the gleaming chest to me with some haste. "You found it, lad. Tis yours to open." Plainly the old buccaneer was afraid of some devilment.

Slowly, I unlatched the clasp and pulled the top gently up. The two lanterns were eagerly thrust forward. "What in blazes?" exclaimed Long John.

Half a dozen thin-walled cups and bowls presented themselves to us, in the most marvelous gold and scarlet colors, with dainty rocks and orchids painted on them, and creamy white inside. Beside them, intricately carved pieces of ivory and a soapy greenish mineral reposed on bundles of the finest silk, shimmering in golds and blues and reds. Our entire company was struck quite dumb at the brilliance of the chest's contents, and for several moments the only sound was the water dripping off the cavern's walls.

Then it struck my sluggish mind where I'd seen the strange markings before. In the Squire's library. On the bottom of his precious blue-and-white China bowls and cups.

"Long John–those markings are Chinese," I whispered.

He looked up at me, puzzlement on his face. "Chinese?"

"Chinese," I affirmed.

"Mate, we're a might far piece from China," he informed me. "But I do hear that they're awfully fond of jade," he allowed, picking up one of the green carved pieces, a delicate landscape scene of rocks and pines, all wonderfully carved in miniature.

"What's that on the bottom of the chest?" Isaiah asked, pushing the silk aside.

"Not so fast, my friend," Silver said sharply. "These here pieces may end up being more valuable than the silver bars. And considerably more fragile, says I."

So saying, he removed the bundles of silk, spread them on the dirt floor, and gently lifted and placed the cups, bowls, and carvings on them. Sure enough, as Isaiah's sharp eyes had observed, a stone tablet rested at the bottom of the chest. Silver hooked a finger under one edge and lifted it with a grunt.

The tablet, perhaps two foot on a side, was covered with much more of the strange Chinese writing on the left half, engraved into the stone. On the right side was what looked like a map, with some 20 ships engraved, and a line running through it.

At the top, above all, were engraved four strange objects, pointed at each end.

"Long John," said I, the hair rising on my neck.

His big faced looked up at me, puzzled, his eyes bulging.

"In Billy Bones' sea chest," I whispered. "He's got five or six seashells. And four of them look just like these." I put my finger on the four objects at the top of the tablet.

His eyes got even bigger. "Why, shiver me timbers," said Long John Silver.

Chapter Five. Billy Bones' Sea Chest

(In Billy Bones' sea chest were)...five or six curious West Indian shells. It has often set me thinking since that he should have carried about these shells with him in his wandering, guilty, and hunted life. –Ch. 4, Treasure Island, *Robert Louis Stevenson*

Glad I was to see Treasure Island disappear behind us that night. I devoutly wished never to lay eyes on the accursed island again. The silver bars were aboard, the crew's third of the bars parceled individually to each, with Taino having an extra share, and Long John's and my third stowed away deep in the bilge as ballast.

The strange Chinese chest resided in Long John's cabin, on his desk beside the sextant and chronometer. On the first night away from Treasure Island, with our course and the watches set, Long John and I pulled out the old, battered sea chest of Billy Bones and opened it. Indeed, the contents were but little changed from that horrible night a year ago, when my mother and I first opened the chest, with Billy Bones lying dead on our parlour floor below us, and Mad Dog and Blind Pew and the rest of Silver's old shipmates swarming towards the Admiral Benbow like maggots to a corpse.

On top was an unworn set of rough cotton clothes over a battered quadrant, several sticks of tobacco, two brace of handsome pistols–I could see Long John coveting those pistols with his fierce eyes. But his respect–

nay, fear–of the dead pirate kept his restless hands from quite claiming them, though how his fingers twitched! An old Spanish watch next, long since run down. A pair of brass-mounted compasses, and then, lying on an old, salt-whitened boat-cloak–

"By the powers," Silver whispered as five seashells came to view. His eager hands, denied the pistols, claimed the shells and laid them on his dark teak desk. The largest shell was the common conch, whose meat sailors love as a diversion from salt pork and turtle jerky. The other four shells were quite different, being smaller and symmetrical, pointed on each end and fuller in the middle. These shells were covered with waves of gold lines in the shape of tents jammed close to each other, so thick in places as to nearly obliterate the white background of the shell. The markings reminded me of distant ranges of mountains.

Long John lay the four shells atop the stone tablet from the Chinese chest.

"An exact fit, to be sure," he whispered, in awe.

I began fiddling with the shells, arranging all four so they sat securely, with the edge of the last whorl of the shell resting on the table. So positioned, they exactly presented the same aspect as engraved on the stone tablet.

"Jim, lad, that's mighty prettily done, to be sure, and they nicely mirrors the engraving. But what the devil does it all mean?" Long John asked.

"Did Billy Bones never mention the shells in his conversation?" I asked.

"Never in his conversation," returned Long John. "But 'twas a jest among the crew how often he and Cap'n Flint would enquire about seashells at every landing and grogshop they saw, from Caracas to Savannah. The Cap'n would quaff his first rum–first o' many, you may lay to it–then heave a great sigh as the stuff warmed his gut, lean those big arms o' his on the bar, and fix the barkeep with his burnin' blue eyes. 'Got any pretty seashells for my mates and me?' he'd ask in that wheezing voice o' his."

"No."

"By the powers, yes. Ye'd think seashells was made of gold, the way those two sought 'em. But 'twere the strangest thing. For all their enquiring, they most always declined the shells offered 'em." He picked up the conch. "This here shell–I've seen Billy and Flint toss aside dozens. Toss 'em on the floor, after eagerly enquiring for 'em."

"Ever see them toss any of these aside?" asked I, touching the smaller shells.

"Nay. Nary a one. For that matter, I didn't see where they put their hands on these. These type shells–ye hardly ever sees 'em."

"Well, I think we know why they were eager for seashells, and why they tossed the bulk of them," said I, running my finger along the engraved shells of the stone tablet.

"Do we? The picture on the tablet ain't that pretty, Jim, to set their hearts aflame, and you may lay to that. These four shells may be unusual, and those wavy gold lines easy on the eyes–but they ain't treasure, my boy."

"That I can't deny, Long John. But you may be sure that Bones and Flint weren't seeking these shells for their beauty. What interested those two in life?"

"Women, rum, and treasure, by thunder. Nothing more nor less."

That judgment seemed to ring true for Long John as well, I thought. "We can rule out women and rum," I said aloud. "These shells have something to do with treasure."

"You mean the jade and porcelain and silk in the chest? I admit that's a slice of treasure, but only a thin slice. What do these here shells have to do with those fineries?"

"I don't know, Long John. But Billy Bones and Flint searching for the shells, and Bones carting them around in his sea chest for all those years–that, with the engraving of just these shells on the tablet here–there's a connection, Long John, and it's got something to do with treasure. More treasure than this little teaser of a chest, here."

He was shaking his head. "I'm no Dutchman, boy. I 'spect my mind is sharper 'n most. But I can't figure it out. Though I think I know who might."

"Who would that be?" I asked quickly.

"This here writing on the tablet be Chinee-writing. I've heard an old

Chinaman lives in Havana, as I rec'lect. Lived there forever, from what I understand. Got a granddaughter or some sich with him. Maybe he can make something of this writing."

"And make our connection," I ventured. "I've wanted to see Havana for many a month, Long John, from studying Havana Bay on the maps in my room."

"Aye, my lad, it's a grand harbor and a grand sight, you may lay to that. In four days, we'll be there." With that, Long John scooped up the four shells and gently deposited them on the unworn cotton clothes atop Billy Bones' sea chest, cast a longing glance at the brace of pistols just below, then closed the chest.

* * * * *

Actually, a good wind pushed us to Havana in three and a half days. Long John had just finished his noon latitude reading on my sextant when the crows nest hailed land. An hour later, the imposing fortress called Del Morro Castle was on our port, sprawling grandly atop a high cliff. The narrow mouth of Havana Bay appeared just beyond the fortress. We sailed through the mouth, another fortress called La Punta Castle on our starboard, heading straight toward the La Fuerza Castle inside the harbor.

The masts of a hundred ships or more crowded the sky of the bay, flying flags from a dozen countries. Galleons from Seville, bilanders from Holland, galiots from France, schooners and ketches from the British colonies in North America, sloops and cutters and more. We yielded to a trio of tugs which grabbed our lines and hauled us to an open area in the bay, with the wharves of the city stretching to our starboard.

Scarcely had we weighed anchor when a longboat from the wharves shot toward us. At its head a large man in a crisp cream uniform sat stiffly erect, with sword and medals gleaming in the afternoon sun, a sweeping blue broad-brimmed hat atop his head.

Long John growled. "I don't often pine for the old life of cuttin' and rippin', Jim. But that big one there makes me wish I had a sharp cutlass in me hand and no witnesses handy, says I. Unfortunately, that be the Commandante, in charge of Del Morro Castle, and the harbor to boot. But I keep dreaming of a dark alley with just him and me."

Hardly was the boat beside us when the Commandante was aboard with half a dozen of his men. "Silver! Your presence, sir!" he yelled as he climbed aboard in awkward, jerky movements. His voice was surprisingly high-pitched for such a large man. The voice would be comical, were it not for the brutal face, the large nose and lips. A scrupulously trimmed ringbeard gleamed around the hard-set mouth.

Long John took his time getting from the poop deck to the port bulwarks.

"Commandante," he said, with a stiff inclination of his head.

"Search the ship, Lieutenant Sanchez," the big Spaniard said to a fat soldier who had just been shoved aboard over the railings from below. The fat one gathered his footing, saluted quickly, then huffed below with his men. The Commandante was surveying the crew with undisguised disgust on his expressive face as he leaned against the edge of the poop deck, arms crossed over his medal-strewn chest.

"How such scum manage to sail your ship is a mystery to me, Silver," he said, as if the men did not exist. "Slaves and mestizos. It must be difficult for you, getting competent work from these dregs."

An angry murmur arose from the crew. Silver's voice cut through the chorus.

"They be freed slaves, Commandante, every last man jack of them," he said. "I've never had a better crew, and you may lay to that." The big Spaniard uttered a derisive laugh, still lounging back against the poop deck. He seemed to enjoy the anger he aroused in the crew as he coldly swept his eyes over them. His gaze stopped at Isaiah.

"Ah. The young buck you claimed from the dungeons of Del Morro Castle," he said with a spreading smile. "My man who...entertained him in the dungeons misses this one badly. No one screams quite like him." He threw back his head and laughed.

With an angry roar Isaiah vaulted over the apple barrel on the deck and charged the Spaniard. Before he was halfway there the Commandante had drawn his sword, a peculiar twanging sound filling the air as he freed the short but very sharp weapon. He eagerly stepped forward to impale the charging Isaiah.

Without thinking, I tackled Isaiah as he barreled past me, dragging him to the deck only yards before the big Spaniard. Several of the crew quickly pinned Isaiah down, all the while casting murderous looks at the Commandante.

Long John had stepped between the Commandante and the struggling Isaiah.

"Ye've no call to bait my crew, Commandante," he said hotly.

"I can say what I want, Silver," the Commandante spat back, slowly and reluctantly sheathing his sword. "I am, after all, the master of Havana Harbor and Del Morro Castle. You and your scum would do well not to forget it." He swept his cold glance over the crew again. "Nothing would give me more pleasure than to discover an opportunity to give this black garbage over to my man in Del Morro's dungeons. So watch your step. All of you."

Just then the fat lieutenant huffed up to the big Spaniard, and whispered in his ear. "Where did you obtain the new instruments in your cabin?" the Commandante snapped.

"I've just returned from Bristol, where I picked up me nephew Jim here from my poor dying sister," Silver lied. "His late lamented father being a shipowner there, Jim inherited the instruments, he did." Silver suppressed a catch in his throat at the memory of his lamented sister, and dabbed at his eye before tears could come.

The Commandante's eyes bored into me. "He seems a dull boy. But then, he is English, is he not?"

"Well, the world can only hold so many Spaniards," Long John replied.

"And what do you mean by that?" the man asked, his nostrils flaring.

"My crew and I believe, sir, that the world has more than enough Spaniards," Long John replied.

"Perhaps you do not care to live in a city built by Spain, sir?" the

Commandante spat back, his right hand eagerly patting the big handle of his sword.

"The opportunity to visit with my good friend the Governor-General of Cuba renders your city quite charming, Commandante."

The Commandante turned to the port bulwarks. "See that you adhere to our Spanish rules strictly, Mr. Silver. And try to keep your black and mestizo rabble from mischief." He awkwardly climbed over the bulwarks and disappeared. Behind him, Lieutenant Sanchez had to be assisted over by several soldiers.

"I see what you mean about the Commandante," I observed to Long John after their longboat had pulled away. "If you ever do find him alone, I hope I'm along."

A dry laugh from Long John. "Some day, lad. Some day, he and I will settle our diff'rences. Meanwhile, let's ashore."

He turned to Isaiah, now standing among the men who had pinned him down. "The usual cleaning and harbor duties, Isaiah. And have your men mind their tongues about their recent good fortune, lest the Commandante lay a duty on it. Launch the longboat for Hawkins and meself."

As Isaiah turned away, Long John laid a rough hand on his arm. "And mind you don't run afoul o' the Commandante, me boy. Leave him to me."

Isaiah glared at Silver for a long moment, then nodded.

Silver turned to me, his broad face brightening. "Lad, I have the good fortune to present you Havana, which despite its harbor master, is a charmin' city. After you."

Chapter Six. Meilu's Strange Visitors

On the first page (of Billy Bones' account book) there were only some scraps of writing...then there was 'Off Palm Key he got itt', and some other snatches, mostly single words and unintelligible. I could not help wondering who it was that had 'got itt', and what 'itt' was that he got. –Ch. 6, Treasure Island, *Robert Louis Stevenson*

Grandfather opened the door. His alert, sparkling eyes widened, then filled with tears. I found myself wrapped in his arms, the earthy smell of his cigar enveloping me. We both were crying–it had been a year, after all, since a girl had left this home in Havana for China. Something different had returned–no longer a girl, but not yet a woman. Something waiting to be born, perhaps–into what, I knew not.

After thanking the ancestors for my safe return, we sat at the great table in the center of the reception hall, the sandalwood table that had seen so many large family celebrations for over three centuries. Now we were down to two, the last of the White Pans, my father and mother taken by smallpox but a month before I had left for China.

Grandfather, short and thin, white hair and lined face, sat puffing steadily on a new cigar, listening wordlessly as I told my tale. My journey to Shanghai, encountering the Black Pans, the story of the returning White Pan, the ultimatum from the beautiful, imperious matriarch of the clan.

Fleeing the younger brother's unfortunate death. And the certainty of being pursued by the older brother.

"They will track me here," I finished. "In a week, or a month, or a year. But yes, they will track me here. Of that I am sure."

Grandfather silently reflected on my tale, and finally spoke. "More than revenge for the younger brother, I think, draws them to us." He inclined his head to the ancestor altar behind us, next to *Ma Tsu's* altar. "They want Pan Fulong's ancestor tablet."

"What?"

"Whoever has the tablet has the spiritual energy, the *ch'i*, of the ancestors. They will want that, for the power it would confer upon them." He shook his head. "But how can we fight them? They will have an army of Tankas, the big boat people."

"I can fight, Grandfather." I pulled out the cloisonne pendant from under my shirt, and pressed the ivory ring in its center. As the chains disengaged and the razor edges bloomed along its perimeter, I flung it backhand at one of the wooden pillars running the length of the hall. The pendant flew true and bit deep into the wood.

It took him but a moment to recover. "Very impressive, I'm sure, Meilu. But really–do you think one throwing star will deter the Black Pans and their Tankas?"

"I don't know. But I do know that we cannot give up, even before we begin."

Grandfather sighed, scratched a match on the table, and relit his cigar, rotating it steadily above the flame. His bright eyes watched the smoke rise, then turned to me.

"You are right, my newly-wise granddaughter. Our ancestor Pan Fulong surely would not give up. We are White Pans, after all. The universe is very large and very strange. We will trust in the universe. To provide us unexpected opportunities, perhaps, that will help us defend ourselves when the Black Pans arrive."

I walked to the pillar, and tugged at the star, pleased at how difficult it was to pull from the wood. Grandfather was wise. But old. I would listen to him, but put my trust in myself. *Ma Tsu* would guide me. I glanced at her beside the ancestor altar, sitting dark and serene with the white pearls on her forehead, curls of smoke from the incense rising beside her. *Ma Tsu* had the strength of the sea, and would give it to me.

The sharp edge of the throwing star broke free of the wood. I touched the ivory ring again, watched the blades retract, and attached the disc to the slim chain around my neck again. Yes, the universe was large, and strange. If my eyes were sharp enough, I would find more weapons. But not today, surely. Feeling suddenly very weary, I picked up my bag, and trudged to my room. There, I feasted my eyes on my crickets, my private altar to *Ma Tsu*, my own bed. After lunch, I would settle into my bed and sleep for days.

I had unpacked, and finished lunch with grandfather, when a knock came on our door. Hatuey, our Indian servant, was clearing the dishes, so I went to the door myself, my free hand on the pendant around my neck. As I cautiously opened the door, I was staggered at the motley crew on our threshhold. A tall, one-legged barbarian with hard eyes, tough skin, and an air of authority. Beside him, a barbarian boy, about my age, but smooth-skinned and soft-eyed. To their left, a tall black youth, a smile hovering on his lips. Lastly, an old Taino Indian, with some black blood.

The tall, one-legged man enquired if Grandfather could translate some "Chinee-writing," as he put it, for them. A few minutes later, we were all seated in the reception hall, where the tall, one-legged one took the lead.

"Much obliged to you for letting us state our problem, Mr. Pan. I be Long John Silver, newly settled in the Vinales Valley southwest of here. Me and my mates but recently run across a stone tablet with some Chinee writing on it. Having heard of you, I thought you might be able to translate for us, to satisfy our curiosity, in a manner of speaking. We will pay handsome for your kindness, you may be sure."

I caught my breath as he mentioned a stone tablet. My glance darted to Grandfather, and saw him slowly take a draw of his cigar, to calm himself. "You will pardon my poor English," he said. "It is my least proficient language, but I hope it will suffice. May I see this stone tablet?" He drew a side table close to him.

The one-legged man pulled the tablet from a bag he carried, and gave it to the boy. My eyes recognized the tablet long before it was placed on the table. Another draw on his cigar by grandfather, quite leisurely. He was thinking very hard and very quickly.

"I will be completely honest with you," he finally said. "This stone tablet was brought here–to this very room–eight years ago. By an exceedingly rough and commanding man. I translated it for him, and he left and we've not seen him since. The contents of the tablet are astonishing. They in fact persuaded me to send my granddaughter here on a most perilous journey. I must enquire if you are willing to hear what the tablet says."

"Willing and eager, by thunder. I likes your honesty, sir," answered the one-legged man. "That man eight years ago was doubtless Captain Jack Flint, the old buccaneer. We've been, ah, quite fortunate, to discover where he hid his treasure, this tablet among it. We've a mind to delve a bit deeper into it all, that we have."

Grandfather looked them over. He shrugged, then turned his old eyes toward me.

"This is my granddaughter, Meilu. She will translate." I picked up the tablet, and spoke slowly, for the Chinese was the old style, and my English was but little better than my Dutch. And it had been eight years, after all, since I had held the tablet.

"*The eighteenth year of the reign of the Yong Le Emperor of the glorious Ming Dynasty*–that would be over three hundred years ago," I explained, "the year 1421 by your calendar–*I, Admiral Zhou Yen of the fleet of the Imperial Head eunuch Zheng He, have returned the barbarian kings and caliphs to their homelands after the inauguration of the Forbidden City, entertaining them with concubines and foods of our great Chinese civilization, and granting each a substantial parting gift of the treasure in our holds.*

"To spread the brilliance of our culture, I was commanded to venture beyond Africa to further barbarian lands. Accordingly, my fleet of 20 treasure ships sailed west from Africa, across the small sea to these fair but treacherous islands. We encountered several islands with particularly savage barbarians–that would be the Carib Indians, on Dominica and Guadeloupe," I pointed out–"*and, departing them, charted two heavily-forested islands*–Hispaniola and Puerto Rico, doubtless–*before finally splitting the fleet to chart both sides of a large island*–that would be Cuba–*but the 12 ships on the north coast*

were soon forced away from the island and half were damaged beyond repair by the abundant reefs and shoals–"

"Aye," interrupted the one-legged man. "That'd be the Great Bahama Bank, says I–many a ship has foundered on that stretch, north o' Cuba."

"*–and we have put into this small, flat island where the shoals meet the great strait separating us from the mainland of Fusang to the north and west.*"

"Andros Island? Or North Bimini, farther north, next to the Florida Strait?" guessed the one-legged man. "By the powers! Flint would hang out on North Bimini, in the old days, he would!"

I continued. "*The ships charting the south coast of the large island, which rendezvoused with us here, report a large bay just around the western tip of the island on the north shore. With abject apologies to the Yong Le Emperor for my unworthy abilities, I cannot take all the sailors, concubines, and treasure from the six heavily damaged ships onto the remaining ones. There is no alternative but to leave some behind. The sailors and concubines we will leave on the shore of the large bay under the command of the able Pan Fulong*"–here my voice choked, at the mention of my White Pan ancestor, abandoned on a strange shore so far from his homeland, over three hundred years ago. I paused, mastered my emotions, and read on.

"*–and the Emperor's treasure from the six damaged ships we will convey to a spot on these islands where it will remain well-hidden, until a rescue convoy can return from China, to reclaim the treasure and the colonists we leave behind. But mindful that I am 100,000 li from our glorious homeland, and that many perils await us still, I also will encode the site of the treasure on a separate device–four shells of the cone that stings–in a hidden manner, so that only the clever mind of one of our race could discover the secret location. The four shells I will furthermore scatter, so that only the determined and resourceful of our race could hope to reclaim them for the prize.*

"*May the sea-goddess Ma Tsu guide and protect me and my remaining crew. I also invoke her good fortune for the sailors and concubines I must leave behind on the shore of the bay of the large island. Zhou Wen, Admiral.*"

Silence gripped the reception room as I finished. I returned the tablet to the table.

The first voice was that of the barbarian boy. "Is it possible, sir, that you and your granddaughter here might be–it scarcely seems possible–the remnant of that colony?"

Another very long draw on the cigar. Grandfather was deciding how much to tell this strange company. He shrugged.

"Why not? Yes. Until we first saw the tablet, eight years ago, all we had were half-forgotten tales of Pan Fulong. *Ma Tsu*, the sea-goddess, we remembered also, but little else. You would be surprised how much a people can forget in three hundred years. The colonists left behind prospered for the first hundred years, enriching our blood with that of the able Taino Indians already here, adopting their manioc and yams. Then the scourge of the Spaniards arrived. They obliterated the fierce Carib Indians on the southern islands–the only good to have come from the Spaniards. But they also very nearly obliterated the Taino here as well, through unprovoked cruelty and massacres.

"Our ancestors, they left alone–both because we were relatively few by then, and because we gave them water from our spring here at our home, before we realized their cruelty. But the Spanish brought diseases as well, which wiped out all but a remnant of us, as well as the remaining Taino."

He paused, and tended his cigar. "My son and his half-Indian wife were taken by one of the Spanish diseases a little over a year ago. Only their daughter here, and myself, remain from the Chinese colony of three hundred years ago. The tablet provided us a possible key to the history of our colony. To the history of our family. Meilu has just returned from China, where she learned the truth of the tablet's claims–and much more."

I noticed a tear running down the cheek of the old Taino Indian as grandfather finished the sad tale of his people and ours.

"Ah, and a might tragic and stirring tale that be, to be sure," said the one-legged man. "But if I may, could we return to the treasure part, Mr. Pan?"

Grandfather sighed, being well-used to the shallowness of barbarians. "What you call 'the treasure part' is lost, Mr. Silver, without the four cone shells pictured on the tablet. Only on them–somehow–is the location of the treasure indicated."

"Aye, and it be right fortunate for us that we has them shells, then," said the one-legged man.

My heart jumped. Grandfather leapt from his chair. "You have the shells?"

"And very safely stowed they be, too, on my ship, sir."

"How in the world did you recover four cone shells scattered three centuries ago throughout the Caribbean?" I blurted. Grandfather frowned at my impetuous question, but turned for the answer.

"It wasn't rightly us as collected them," the one-legged man explained. "That old buccaneer as visited you eight years ago devoted the last years of his short, wicked life to scouring the Caribbean for them shells. While he twarn't partic'lar polite about his methods, he be wondrously thorough. From Caracas to Palm Key to Savannah he had but one question for every spot he touched–'Have ye any pretty seashells for me friends?' he'd say, in that winning manner of his. Many a useless shell he tossed, conches and sich, but in the end, he had the four engraved on this here tablet. And now they be sitting on me own ship, what be christened *Pieces of Eight*, and if that ain't the proper name I don't know what might be!" The one-legged man, at that, burst into raucous laughter.

Grandfather, still standing, was so shocked and intrigued he forgot to even draw on his cigar. He took it from his mouth and let it burn as he thought. "So. You have the shells," he finally said, sitting down. "Good luck to you. Please leave a doubloon on the table as you depart, for the translation." He nudged the tablet toward the barbarians.

"Begging your pardon, Long John," said the boy. "It strikes me that we'll be wanting yet another duty from the gentleman."

"What might that be?" snapped the other.

"The tablet doesn't tell us the secret of the shells," he began. "Only that the secret is somehow coded in the shells. And further, mores the pity, that it will take a great deal of cleverness–indeed, Chinee-cleverness–to tease the secret out of the shells."

"Aye, that be so," the one-legged man admitted, peevishly. His greed for the treasure had put him out of sorts.

"Would it not be advisable, nay necessary, for us to enlist the aid of this gentleman in unlocking the secret of the shells, Long John?"

The one-legged man stood, and hobbled about on his crutch. Thinking was plainly difficult for him, as for many barbarians. Finally he sat. "How much would ye want, sir, for providing help with the shells?" he said bluntly.

"We have reason to believe our input might be critical," grandfather said quietly.

"All right. Ten shares per a hundred. That be generous," the other snapped.

Grandfather shook his head, and took another draw on his cigar. He examined it as he held the smoke, noting how close he was to the end. Then exhaled. "I doubt you can find it without our assistance. So ten percent seems low. But my granddaughter and I are content, and our needs few. We will help you for a mere quarter of the treasure."

"Done, by thunder!" shouted the one-legged man. "And we'll all be rich for it, of that you may be sure!"

"Meilu," Grandfather said. I bowed. "Pack a few things, and accompany these gentlemen to their ship. Do whatever it takes to unlock the secret and find the treasure."

The others did not hide their consternation. "Now see here, my good sir. We expect your assistance, not your granddaughter's," the one-legged man blustered.

Grandfather stubbed out his cigar in a conch-shell ashtray. "My granddaughter is every bit as intelligent as I. But she is much more experienced than myself. I have never left this island. She returned this morning from a year in China. She is the person for you."

The one-legged man was speechless, an event that happened rarely, I imagined.

"She's been to China?" he finally stammered. "How?"

"When we first read the tablet eight years ago, I needed confirmation," answered Grandfather. "It seemed to give us the secret of our family history. But was it true? For seven years, we gathered resources, and let her mature and grow in knowledge and abilities. A year ago, not long after the unfortunate death of her parents from smallpox, she signed as a sailor on a ship east to Veracruz, disguised as a boy. Crossed Mexico, to Acapulco. She sailed on a galleon from there to Manila, and from there to China. For six months she explored that great land, from her base in Shanghai. Then the return trip. This young lady has emerged successful from more adventures than most of us in this room. She's the person to help you unlock the secret of the cone shells and find the treasure."

"Did she learn why the rescue convoy never came?" asked the boy. His mind, I could see, cut to the heart of things.

All turned to me. "While Zhou Wen and the rest of the eunuch Zheng He's fleet sailed to the far corners of the world in 1421," I said, "a great fire destroyed the newly built Forbidden City, and epidemics raged in the south. Emperor Yong Le's mandate from heaven was shattered. The mandarins took over the government, destroyed Zhou Wen's maps when he returned, and China's great ships were grounded. To this day."

"Ah. A tragic tale, to be sure," the one-legged man said impatiently. "But here ye be, and here we be. How long might it take you to gather your things, young lady?"

I stood. "I will meet you in the entry courtyard in ten minutes," I stated, and swept out of the hall. I fought back tears, but they came as I reached my room. I shut my door, and stood weeping, silently, the tears flowing like rain down my cheeks. Not so much at leaving my room and my precious belongings, even though I'd only been back a matter of hours. But below that, so deep I couldn't even see there, I was changing from a girl to a woman–without the slightest clue as to what that meant. I could feel...something happening. Something strange stirring inside me, wanting to be born. But without my mother to guide me, I had no knowledge what it was, and how it would somehow bloom into life. I didn't even have a sister–not even a female friend!–to talk with about the mysterious events happening deep inside me. Instead, here I was, assigned to leave everything behind again, and join yet another company of males–*barbarian* males at that!

I angrily threw some clothes, a cape, an extra hat, into my traveling bag. I looked around my room. No! Some things I would not abandon so soon after regaining them. I grabbed the bamboo cage containing my favorite cricket, the one with the sweet bell-like peal. My Seven Board pieces. And a large packet of tea. Do barbarians have hot water?

I stood straight, the bag across my shoulder. I wiped the tears from my cheek. This was for my family. The White Pans. Grandfather. Mother and father, lost a year ago. And all the other ancestors stretching back in time, to Pan Fulong here in Havana, and his ancestors left behind in Shanghai. I lit a fresh stick of incense in my altar to *Ma Tsu* the sea-goddess. *Help me, Ma Tsu. Help me cope with the mystery waiting to be born within me.* Bowing to the altar, I fought back more tears, steeled myself against my loneliness, and with one last look at my room, headed for the entry courtyard and the strange company of my new companions.

Halfway to the courtyard, the barest suggestion that this bizarre company of barbarians might be our hoped-for gift from the universe floated through my mind. I uttered a disgusted laugh at the notion. A boy, a one-legged man, a slave, and an Indian.

Not much of a gift.

Chapter Seven. Tabitha Escapes

I'm there already, hidden in shadows of the deep window alcove high on the wall in the study of Don Gabriel, Count of Jaruco. *Obatala* helps me be invisible. The Commandante enters, crisp uniform, gleaming ringbeard, short sword at his side. Just as on that horrible day, when he convinced his mistress to banish my mother to the plantations. Then killed her with his sword when she fought. He is handsome outside, cruel inside. The kind of man who enjoys cutting Xavier on the face, then hanging him in the cage by the Ceiba tree.

He and Don Gabriel meet every week here in the count's grand house on the Plaza Vieja. Conversation, as always, is of male things. The horse races that afternoon, which jockey would throw the race, profits from wagers. Commandante's new mistress, her many charms. Happenings in Seville, how to profit from new regulations. Their cigar smoke rises to the window. It swirls and dips, showing the presence of unseen spirits in the room.

He will be harder to kill than I thought. Perhaps my old plan–walk into the barber shop, and shoot him with a stolen pistol–would work. But I am not so sure, now, without Xavier to distract the barber. I need to learn more about the Commandante and his habits. Learn what he does and where he goes. Perhaps there is a better way, a better place. Someday, perched in the shadows of a room, I'll overhear something I can use.

I haven't moved for twenty minutes. Staying absolutely still is my secret, along with my dark cloak and dark face. And *Obatala's* help. My months on the street have taught me. Men can look right at you, but not notice, if you are hidden and unmoving. How many conversations I've overhead. How much food I've stolen. When I do move, it is fast and without stop. Not impulsively, like Xavier. That was his weakness. I consider before I move. But there are times when you must be fast. I am an extreme. Absolutely still, or absolutely quick. *Absolutely alone, too. Without momma.*

Being thin helps. Their conversation winding down, I squeeze under the outside bars guarding the window, past the house martin nest. I grab the gutter, and slide down the stucco wall. As my feet touch dust, I glide into the Plaza Vieja fronting the Count's palace.

It's market day in the Plaza. Peasants flow into the huge square, live pigs slung over their shoulders, squirming. Chickens held upside down by their feet, squawking. Parrots and monkeys everywhere. The vendors are freed slaves, who know me. No need to steal food from them. Pineapples, bananas, strips of dried meat are freely given. An old Mandinka woman beside a heap of fruit touches my shoulder. She points back. The Commandante, emerging from the huge wooden door under the Jaruco coat of arms, is headed straight for me, though no notice yet.

I quickly kneel beside the seated woman's legs, and arrange my cloak over her dark, flowing skirt. And over me. I crouch low, and don't move.

The Commandante approaches. I can imagine his restless eyes, roaming, searching. For escaped slaves, including me. It is his passion in life, to send the condemned back to hell.

"How much for the *mamey colorado*?" I hear him ask the Mandinka woman. He is standing beside her. And me.

"Two *reales*, Commandante," she whispers, more fearful than me.

"Put it on my tab," I hear him smirk, walking away with one of the fruits.

A moment. "He is gone," the woman whispers.

I wait another moment, then am moving. She tosses me a *mamey*. "On your tab," she grins, as I pocket it.

I walk through the market, admiring bacon, pineapples, eggs, flowers. I am opposite the house of the beautiful Cardenas sisters. Remembering the brightly lit party there last week–bright lights a challenge for me, the dark, unmoving one.

"Hey! You!" The Commandante's voice. I look toward the sound. He's pointing at me, directing his fat lieutenant and two nearby soldiers.

Foolish carelessness! *Obatala, help me now.* Already moving, I dash up Mercaderes Boulevard running north from the plaza. The street is crowded with people, donkeys, and carts headed for the market. I dodge around a cartload of flowers, golden irises and purple bougainvillea. Twist through a dozen peasants carrying baskets of pineapples. Scramble under a wagon laden with strong-smelling *tasajo* strips of turtle meat. The cream-colored oxen shy away from my movement, nearly tipping the wagon. The Commandante and more of his men are still close, though. Unusual for soldiers to be so strong. A high stack of hay hides the donkey under it, and me for a second or two. My legs are tiring. Ahead on the left is the huge carved door of the Casa de la Obra Pia palace, a slave milking a goat there. Should I dash into the open doorway? I have friends among its slaves. But no. It would be my coffin if the soldiers saw me enter it.

I cannot outrun the Commandante and his soldiers. They are still close behind me. I grasp the amulet of *Obatala* around my neck in desperation. *Obatala* gives me a vision. The great Ceiba silk-cotton tree in the Plaza de Armas. I see Momma and me leaving fruit and lighting candles to the *orisha* of the tree every day. I see Xavier's cage hanging from the tree's lowest branch. The tree calls me.

At the top of Mercaderes, I careen right onto the gray cobblestones of Calle Obispo. I trip on the rough cobblestones, but quickly pick myself up. Soon I burst into the Plaza de Armas, the Ceiba tree towering at its harbor end. But there are even more soldiers here. A knot of them loiter in front of the La Fuerza castle ahead on the left. I'm cut off in front. The Commandante is about to turn the corner into the square behind me. *I'm trapped, Obatala.*

I slip behind a palm tree, panting hard, and find myself staring into a strange group who've just entered the square also. A one-legged man, a boy, a slave, Yoruba like me, I think. An old man, Taino Indian. And a girl, a race unknown to me, wide slanting eyes. Behind them towers the Ceiba tree, framing them. Pointing to them.

I hear the Commandante enter the square, shouting orders to his men. The eyes of the strange group go from me, panting, to the Commandante. Back to me, hidden for the moment by the palm tree. I stare defiantly back at them, rubbing the amulet of *Obatala* for luck. I realize they cannot possibly save me. I prepare to dash away, though it will reveal me to the Commandante and his soldiers. *I am dead. Soon I will join Xavier's bones in the cage.*

Suddenly the girl of the strange eyes reaches into a bag over her shoulder. She pulls out a brilliant gold cloak, and throws it over my shoulders. I cringe under the brightness, the color. A broad hat next, onto my head. Then she steps close to me. The tall slave steps to the other side of me. The one-legged man next, then the Indian. Last, the boy, reluctant. I am brilliant in color, part of a larger group. The Commandante rushes up, panting.

"Silver! Did you see her?" His eyes dart around, everywhere but the group surrounding me.

"The dark slave girl, you mean?" the one-legged one answers.

"Yes! Yes!"

"She slipped over that wall toward the Plaza de Cathedral," the one-legged one says, pointing right. "Can she ever jump! Just swarmed over it, by the powers!"

"Yes! She's the very devil. A dark, wily devil. But now I have her! That's a blocked alley behind the wall. This way, men!"

He races towards the wall, directing men right and left.

"Thanks, Silver!" he calls over his shoulder.

"Happy to be of service, I'm sure," the one-legged one says quietly.

Again quietly, but to me, now. "Whoever you are–stay in the middle of us. Everyone–we're walking slowly to the harbor, we are. It's only a block's worth, through the square, but it's our heads–and this girl's, too–if we appear to hurry."

I have not moved so slow for two months. We pass the great Ceiba tree. I solemnly bow to it with gratitude for my escape. I ache to see momma there, lighting a candle to the ancient spirit of the tree. But no. She is gone. We pass the cage, where Xavier died. Soon we are at the nearby dock, and climb into a longboat. The Indian and the slave lock oars.

"Take us around to the far side of *Pieces of Eight*, Isaiah, Taino," the one-legged one says, quietly. "The Commandante will soon realize he lost her somewhere, and I don't want him eyeing us as he's casting about for where that happened."

On the far side of the ship, we climb aboard, hidden. The girl of the strange eyes takes me by the elbow.

"Don't touch me!" I hiss, wrenching my elbow free. They have saved me, but my distrust is deep.

Her eyes widen, but her hand drops. We walk with the others down stairs, into a large room under the deck. Light streams in from a window. I am trembling. The room is too bright. My clothes are too bright. But the clothes, and the people in the room, have saved my life. I am not in the cage with Xavier's bones.

I bow before them, knee bent. "I owe you my life. Thank you." My momma's mistress had an English lover, before the Commandante, so I know something of their language.

The one-legged man takes the big hat off my head. He tosses it onto a table, where strange instruments cluster.

"Stand up, me hearty, and let's a look at ye." His voice is booming, full of life. "You're an enemy of the Commandante, so that makes you a friend of mine. But, mate, you've a might lot of explaining to do, I reckon."

I sway. I am strong, but everything is bearing down on me. It is too much.

"Take this seat," the girl of the strange eyes says to me, a gentle command in her voice. I gratefully collapse into the chair she slides near me. A glass of rum is thrust in my hand by the one-legged man.

"This will help, dearie. Even if you ain't accustomed to it, it'll clear your head wondrously."

A sip. He's right. It burns, but it sharpens my mind.

"Whenever ye be ready, matie," the one-legged man says.

All are seated in chairs around me. They seem kind, but I am always suspicious, always expecting cruelty. I calculate the chances of escaping from the room. They are very small. And I do owe these people my life. I have not relaxed in so long. I have not been truthful in so long. Tears rush to my eyes. It is very hard to let my guard down, to speak simple truth. Tears flowing down my face, I give up.

"My mother named me Tabitha," I begin. "My father died on the slave ship. We ended up with the wife of a shipowner. My mother was her personal servant. But she tired of mother's pride. And the Commandante convinced her to send us to the plantations."

A gasp from most. They too know the plantations are death for the slaves.

"Momma refused to let me go to the plantations. Said she owed my life to my dead father. She fought so I could escape. She was killed, by the Commandante, as she fought. I've lived on the streets for two months, now. Survived, by learning how to become invisible. To melt into darkness. There is much darkness in the world. On streets, in sewers, even in a normal room. I've overheard many conversations of the Commandante, from high windows and dark corners. I am learning his habits and secrets, so I can kill him some day. I *will* avenge my momma. I have sworn this on the amulet of *Obatala* which I wear." I finger the bundle momma tied around my neck in the room under the stairs. Unlike much of this world, it is white and pure. It protects me from the darkness. The world of the *orisha* is not like this world.

Silence. They do not believe me. I check the exits from the cabin, again gauging my chances for escape.

"What do ye know of the Commandante?" the one-legged man asks abruptly. He is testing me.

"What horse he'll wager on this afternoon–*Lightning Bolt*," I answer. "His current mistress–*Countess Esperanza*. What days he sees her–*Tuesday* and *Friday*, occasionally *Sunday*, if her husband is away. What presents he brings her–*Encantadora*, her favorite perfume, this week. Where he drinks in the evenings–*the Silver Palace*. Where he gambles through the nights–well, dozens of places. Who shaves him and trims his ringbeard–*the barber Felipe off Avenida Aguiar*. How often he changes his shirt–*twice a day*. His favorite restaurants–again, dozens. Today he ate at *The Golden Cockerel*."

"By thunder, I likes that!" the one-legged man roars, hitting the table with his open hand. He laughs loudly. "You're a likely lass," he says between laughs, "though a might thin, and haughty as a princess in your manner. No matter. I'll adopt you onto this here ship, and you may lay to that! We'll hunt the Commandante together, you and me."

The girl of the strange eyes takes the hat from the table. "Captain Silver. Do you have a cabin that you could devote to your female guests?"

The one-legged man looks to the old Indian. "Taino? Would ye care to move in here with me, matey, and let the two ladies have your cabin?"

The old Indian nods.

"This way, ladies," the one-legged man says. He pushes himself off his chair and onto his crutch. "Your *suite* awaits you. And a better haven for sisters ye cain't imagine, I'll wager."

I rise, and suddenly the cabin tilts, and begins to blur. The girl takes my arm again, steadies me. I twist my arm away from her grasp. I am not used to kindness, and do not know what she might want from me. I have nothing to give. Nothing. All I have is my hatred for the Commandante. And my momma's amulet of *Obatala*. Nothing else. I am strong, though thin, and tall for my age. I am Yoruba. I am *Obatala's* servant. And I *will* have my revenge on the Commandante someday. With or without anyone's help.

Chapter Eight. Mute Shells

I miss my old home in the alley with Xavier. This ship is never still, always pitching and rolling, as if the *orishas* of the sea were angry. Too much movement. The girl of the strange eyes–Meilu, she says she is called–constantly watches me, as though she needs something from me. But I cannot give anything to anyone.

Why can't she see this? She tries to help me set up a corner of the room as my own. I push her away, and sit trembling on the bed. I watch her adorn her part of the room. A statue on a table, incense before it. The statue is of a woman–black face, I see with surprise, pearls on her forehead. The strange-eyed girl bows before it, and lights incense. Like me and momma lighting candles before the *orisha* of the Ceiba tree. At least she knows the world is alive with unseen spirits. That we must honor these spirits, so they will help us. It is a dangerous world we live in. We must have help from the spirits.

"Time for the big meeting," says the boy as he sticks his face in the door. Even though he is English and not Spanish, I do not like him. He smiles much too easily, to the others at least. Doesn't he know how dangerous the world is? How full of disappointments? To us–me, and the strange-eyed girl–he is cold, though. Unsmiling. He does not like us, or trust us. He is like me, towards us. Because of this, I have more trust of him than the others. I have learned. That one who shows his dislike for you is more trustworthy than one who pretends to like you.

We gather in the one-legged man's large room. He is there, with the boy, the strange-eyed girl, and the black slave they call Isaiah. And me, though I do not belong here, or anywhere.

All their eyes are on the table. Complicated pieces of metal sit there, things sailors use to find their position. And an old stone tablet, with strange carvings on it. Ships and islands and strange writing. The outline of four shells. And just above the carved shells sit actual shells, golden and white and beautiful. The shells remind me of *Obatala*–white and pure and clean. Not of this world. All eye the four shells with awe. As if they were heavier, more real, than everything else.

"The shells, they hold the key to a treasure," the strange-eyed girl whispers to me. "We are trying to find how their message is hidden, so we can be guided to the treasure."

I have no use for treasure. But these people have saved me from the Commandante. If I can, I will help them.

"Ye translated the writing on the tablet, my dear," begins the one-legged man, to the strange-eyed girl. "But what of this here map on the right side of the tablet? And by the powers, I've never seen such a number of masts on the ships depicted there."

The girl steps forward. She moves smooth, like water. She puts her finger on the carved ships. "I've sailed on galleons to and from Manila, and never have even I seen ships like these, Captain Silver," she admits. "Admiral Zhou Wen's treasure ships of 1421 each had nine masts and were 480 feet long. They were floating cities, Captain Silver, with a thousand men and women and servants on each ship."

"It strains the imagination, it does," whispers the one-legged man. "And what of the map engraved on this here tablet?"

"Let me guess," the boy says, stepping up to the table. He wants to show his knowledge. "If the Squire's geography lessons have done me any good, this would be China, the beginning of their voyage. Then Siam here. Java, where the Dutch have established themselves. The Gulf of India, various cities. Mombasa on the East Africa coast. Around the Horn of Africa, then across the Atlantic from the Canary Islands."

"God bless the squire," the one-legged man interrupts. "You profited from your lessons with him, that you did."

The boy continues, glowing with pride. He does appear to know much, though he is too aware of it. "This would be Guadaloupe, and Dominica. Then Puerto Rico and Hispaniola, Jamaica to the south. Cuba here, clearly." He pauses.

The one-legged man cuts in. "That be Andros Island, I'll wager. That would make this North Bimini. And the coastline stretching across the Florida Strait would be the North American colonies, by thunder!"

"Which Zhou Wen called Fusang," the strange-eyed girl adds.

"Aye, and we'll drink a toast to the good Admiral for a voyage that makes me head dizzy!" says the one-legged man. "But later, dearie, later. Right now, only one thing keeps me attention." He points to the four shells above the tablet. "These here shells, what be pictured on the tablet, and the treasure they be the key to, by the powers."

We all bend over the shells on the table. Even I am curious. Each shell is about three inches long. Narrow at the bottom, and thicker toward the middle, then tapering quickly to a point at the top. Like the spire of the cathedral west of the Plaza de Armas. The shells are white, covered with shapes outlined in gold, like tents, or mountain peaks, stretching into the distance. Many of them. On the spire of the shells, the mountain peaks disappear, and gold lines curl through the white background. The shells are beautiful. They remind me of *Obatala*, again. I like looking at them.

"Remind me, dearie. What did the tablet call these pretty things?" inquires the one-legged man.

"*The shells that sting*," answers the strange-eyed girl. "Rare here in the Caribbean, but fairly common in the Pacific Ocean. They are easily found in the bay at Manila, where they are called *cone* shells. Many types exist, these being the *'cloth of gold'* cones, for their beauty."

"How so, *sting*?" the boy asks. He picks up a shell.

She shrugs her shoulders. "Apparently they shoot some structure loaded with poison into their prey, which paralyses the fish or worm. Humans handling the shells get the same treatment–often enough it kills them."

The boy quickly drops the shell back onto the desk, to the laughter of all.

"It requires the maker of the shell to still be alive and occupying it," says the strange-eyed girl.

He flushes, and throws an angry look at her. He does not like her. Or me.

"So–to business, as Master Hawkins often reminds us," says the one-legged man. "What be the message these pretty and deadly cone shells be telling us, young Miss Meilu?"

The strange-eyed girl picks up each shell and looks closely at it. She turns the shell in her hands with a sure, steady touch that I like. She brings each shell close to her eyes. Peers at the mountains, and the golden lines on the spire.

"No Chinese characters anywhere–which I expected to find hidden among the wandering lines," she admits, frowning. "Nor any map or directions that I can spot among the lines of any shell." She arranges the shells in a row, as they are engraved on the stone tablet. "Perhaps when put together, they reveal–"

We all eagerly stare at the four shells. Nothing.

She changes the order of the shells in their line and peers at them again. Changes the order several times. Still nothing.

"Turn them upside down, like this," the boy suggests, putting the spires on the bottom. Nothing. Then he rearranges their order in this position. Still nothing.

Gloom settles over the cabin as we stand staring at the gold and white shells. I sense they had expected the secret would be simple to discover. Even I know that nothing is simple in this world. Nothing is easy.

"Methinks we need a change of scenery," the one-legged man says. "And nervous it makes me, it does, to be sitting in the middle of the Commandante's harbor with these here shells." He turns to the tall slave. "Where be the tide, Isaiah?"

"Going out, in half an hour or so, Cap'n Silver."

"Let's be on it, my fine lad. Turn us west beyond the mouth of the harbor. I've a hankering to see my missus, I have." He winks at the boy. They seem to know each other from the past. "And beyond that, I'm wantin' to transfer my share of the silver bars to me plantation basement.

My friends, allow me to sail you to Punta Gorda, and then a brief wagon ride to the Vinales Valley, where you'll enjoy my hospitality and that of my missus while we work on the secret of the shells!"

In an hour we have cleared Havana Bay. We are sailing west down the coast. My only experience with ships is the journey from my homeland on the slave ship. It was five years ago, but I remember it clearly. The smell, the excrement, the vomit, the beatings. I am trembling with the memories. I had my momma, then. Now, I am alone.

The constant rolling of the deck still troubles me. I stand at the front, one hand clutching the rope from the front sail to the ship's point. I have not been out of Havana in our five years here. My heart is beating wildly. I am scared to be leaving the only place I know. But I am joyous at leaving the only place I know, at the same time. And the coastline passing beside us brings old memories, of my homeland. The trees, the beaches, the inland clouds. I am sad, that I am so far from my old home. And joyous, that again I am seeing forests and beaches and clouds.

It is very confusing for me.

I sense a movement behind me. I spin–it is only the boy. He has approached the strange-eyed girl. She bends over something on the deck, her hands flying. She arranges and rearranges some flat pieces of wood. Their shapes are strange. Despite my wariness, I am curious. I unsteadily walk over, grabbing lines and railings as I go.

"What's that?" the boy asks the strange-eyed girl.

"The Seven Board," she answers, her hands not pausing. I see now there are seven pieces of wood. One is a square. Five are triangles, different sizes. The last is like a rectangle that has sagged. She is putting them together in different arrangements. Suddenly a bird appears!

The boy and I gasp in surprise. She looks up, smiling. "What would you like me to make?" she asks me, pulling the bird apart and scattering the pieces again.

"Make?"

"Sure. Anything," she says with another smile. I distrust smiles.

I look around. "A sailing ship," I say, giving her something too difficult to do.

Without a word, she sets to it. Her hands fly again, trying this arrangement of the pieces, then that. Then another. In less time than my momma took to wash my face at night, a sailing ship appears before my eyes!

"How do you do that?" the boy asks, laughing.

"No special technique," she replies. "You just play with the seven pieces. Try this, try that. The fun of it is in the playing with the arrangement of the pieces. You can make anything. Care to try?" she asks us.

I step back, shaking my head.

The boy sits on the deck beside the pieces. He is always ready for adventure, I can see. Not impulsive, like Xavier. But always ready to try things.

"What should I make?" he asks.

"Try something easy. A drunken sailor," she suggests.

He frowns. It is clear he thinks "a man" would not be easy. Much less "a sailor." Much, much less "a drunken sailor." With an annoyed look at her, he begins shoving the pieces around. He tries for five minutes, with no success.

"Can't be done," he announces, shoving the pieces aside angrily.

"You're not having fun with it," she says, in a tone that annoys him even more. "You're making it work. Let it be fun. Just play with the pieces."

She leans over his shoulder, and quickly arranges the seven pieces into–a drunken sailor. It is wonderful.

The boy and I laugh. He wants to dislike the strange-eyed girl. But the game is winning him over.

"Show us again. First, the bird," I say, scrambling the seven pieces on the deck.

For an hour, the boy and I take turns making shapes with the pieces. I have better luck than him. But he is persistent. Soon both of us are making many shapes. Most are awkward, but recognizable as something. The strange-eyed girl says that we are "playing" with the Seven Board. It is like thinking with your hands.

With a shock, I realize I am enjoying myself. I have not enjoyed myself for two months. In the past, I liked being with the other slaves in the kitchen, preparing food. Taking part in their jokes and laughter. The Seven Board is making me forget the Commandante and my momma. I do not want to forget them. But perhaps for a short time, it is permitted. All I think about is the square, the triangles, and the sagging rectangle, which the boy calls a "parallelogram." This is an awkward word. English has none of the beauty of my Yoruban tongue. It is even less pleasing to the ear than Spanish. Though the fact that it is Spaniards speaking Spanish robs the language of any beauty it might have.

Just before sunset we arrive at Punta Gorda–"fat point." We all work together to unload the one-legged man's share of a great pile of silver bars onto a wagon he hires there. It is growing dark as the wagon creaks along the rutted trail toward the Vinales Valley. The one-legged man drives the wagon. I am very lost, and confused again.

We three younger ones sit on the silver bars in the back. Soon the trees and bushes are afire with fireflies, called *cocullos* by the Spaniards. One flutters into the wagon. It lights up our faces, then leaves. I imagine the *cucullo* is an *orisha*, magical and not of this world, visiting us for brief moments. Then gone.

The boy is asleep. I am too excited–and scared–for sleep. The strange-eyed girl and I tell each other about our mothers. The way they smelled. The sound of their voices. How they held us in the dark. We are different, she and I. We are surprised that we remember the same things about our mothers.

Around midnight I hear the one-legged man calling into the darkness. Answers float back. Lights appear–brighter than the *cocullos*–and we roll into the one-legged man's home in the Vinales Valley. African servants greet him happily. He locks the wagon–and his silver–within an inside courtyard, then leads us to the central courtyard.

A chair is carried into the courtyard, resembling a throne. A handsome African lady is seated on it. Her dark face glows with beauty and happiness, particularly when she sees the one-legged man. Yet her hips and legs are shrunk in a strange manner. She is confined to the chair.

The one-legged man surprises us. He plants a gentle kiss on the lady's forehead. "Jim, Meilu, Tabitha," he announces with a glowing face. "I have the pleasure to introduce you to my missus, Lady Silver." At this he bows grandly, and sweeps off his tricorner hat.

We all laugh, including the crippled lady with the radiant face.

"Jim Hawkins I have heard of, often, and if half the stories be half-true, then I am honored," the lady says sweetly. Her voice is smooth, and lilting. "And I look forward to learning more of his two companions."

"T'would be a boon if some modest items of food were able to appear at this late hour, my dear," Long John says to her. "In a word, we be famished."

The radiant cripple, Lady Silver she is called, claps her hands. She speaks a few words to a servant nearby.

My heart stops.

She has spoken in the Yoruban tongue. She has spoken in the tongue of my momma! I stumble towards her, in a daze, Yoruban words falling from my lips. I find myself staggering into her waiting arms, crying. The shock of it is too much for me.

The radiant cripple is stroking my hair, just as momma did. I am sobbing still.

"Lead our other guests to the dining hall, John," she says. "I believe this young lady and I have some talking to do."

Soon we are alone in the courtyard.

"Tell me your story," she says, simply.

I tell her. Everything. It is comforting to speak in my Yoruban tongue. About the voyage over to Cuba, losing my father. Our lives in the shipowner's home. Baking pies in the kitchen with the other slaves. Momma washing my face every night. I cry again, as I tell her of the Commandante, and mother's death. Of my months on the streets. Of impulsive Xavier and his capture by the Commandante. My gift to Xavier. My rescue from the Commandante in the Plaza de Armas by the one-legged man and the others. The stubborn secret of the shells. Even the Seven Board, and *cocullos*. The darkness washes over me.

I awake to birdcall in soft morning light. A servant has placed a basin of water beside my bed. After cleaning my face and brushing my hair, I walk through the house and find the dining hall.

It seems like a dream. So much safety, so much comfort. I must be careful.

The rest–the boy, the strange-eyed girl, the one-legged man and his wife–are already there. The strange-eyed girl has woken early. She has made a new set of Seven Board pieces in the one-legged man's workshop. She gives the boy his own set of pieces.

His eyes tell me he is reluctantly losing his dislike of her.

After a breakfast the one-legged man shows us his tobacco plantation. It is different than the sugar cane plantations that the Commandante was going to send momma to. Here, the slaves are all freed slaves. They seem to freely work, picking, bundling, and drying the huge leaves. The smell in the drying sheds is not like anything I know. It reminds me of leather, soil, and trees, and, for some reason, of the pies in the mistresses' kitchen.

"Long John, I've a mind to take up smoking," the boy says with a laugh. We are standing in one of the drying sheds.

"One of the finer pleasures of life, my boy, and one of the few that don't come back to bite you in some unpleasant way," the one-legged man declares. He is very confident about everything.

One of the drying sheds is hotter than he wants. So the one-legged man and the boy stay behind to work on the stove there. He tells us to return to the house. The radiant cripple will take us to one of the local caves, called *mogotes*. The men will join us there later for lunch. As we leave the shed, the boy flops down on the dirt floor. Soon he is playing with his new Seven Board pieces. The one-legged man wrestles with the stove. He is cursing it heartily as we leave. I have never heard most of the words he is using.

Chapter Nine. Lady Silver's Tale

I forgot to tell you that Silver is a man of substance; I know of my own knowledge that he has a banker's account, which has never been overdrawn. He leaves his wife to manage the inn…she is a woman of colour. (Ltr. from Squire Trelawney to Dr. Livesey) –Ch. 7, Treasure Island, *Robert Louis Stevenson*

It is hard. By *Obatala* it is hard. Here, in this green valley, I am adrift. The landmarks of my life were danger and pain, but at least I knew them. Could count on them, on the streets of Havana. Now–there is too much freedom, too much comfort. Too many new acquaintances who seem to be my friends. But I know the world. You cannot trust things as they seem. You can only trust the *orisha*.

Perhaps, just perhaps, I might trust the crippled wife of the one-legged man, she of the radiant face. The radiant cripple is Yoruba. She knows *Obatala*, and *Chango*, and the other *orishas*. No one can fool the *orishas*. I saw it, in the entrance to her home last night. The bowl of water, a flower floating in it, to welcome the *orishas*, to comfort the spirits of the dead. My momma was there. I could feel her presence.

So maybe the radiant cripple can be trusted. The strange-eyed girl and I are riding in a wagon, driven by the one-legged man's first mate, Isaiah. He is tall, and strong, and laughs much. His teeth are very white. He is not Yoruba, but Mandinka, like the fruit woman in the Plaza Vieja. We arrive at a green hill which hides a cave under it. The *mogote* cave is airy and spacious inside. The white-tooth Mandinka helps the radiant cripple from the wagon. He carries her to a waiting chair in the cave, beside a table. On his next trip, he brings a basket of fruit from the back of the wagon.

The radiant cripple begins to peel *mamey colorado* fruit. Her hands are like her face–strong, and beautiful. Long muscles ripple up her arms as she peels. She is strange, a puzzle. Part of her is beautiful and strong. While part of her is shriveled and useless.

Sometimes I think I am much like that.

She gives some of the red fruit to the strange-eyed girl. A small, delicate box of bamboo is pulled from the girl's pocket. She pushes parts of the fruit into openings of the box.

"*Ha-va-na! Ha-va-na!*" erupts from the box, musical and pleasant.

In spite of myself, I join the others in laughter.

"She is my joy in life, my favorite cricket," says the girl. I have heard the boy, Hawkins, say she is from China. I do not know what, or where, such a place might be.

The cricket in the bamboo box is singing much, now, sitting well-fed on the table. It is pleasant, and I relax a bit.

"Tabitha has told me her sad story, of the loss of her father on the slave ship to Cuba, and the recent loss of her mother," says the radiant cripple, placing some slices of *mamey colorado* on the table before me. "Life is hard, always, particularly for us Yoruba. But I have not heard from you, Meilu, though I have heard from your cricket."

The China girl plays with the cricket cage a bit.

"My life was not so bad, growing up. My mother and father were very kind, and we always had plentiful food, and of course the fresh water from our spring, which we bottle and sell. Our ancestors, abandoned on a strange shore three hundred years ago, remembered enough of our culture to make our lives here rich and full. I was particularly close to my mother–she was mother, and sister, and friend to me."

She puts the box down, and shoves it away from her. "Then the smallpox killed my mother and father. In a week, I went from a full family to only Grandfather. It was like a dream–a very bad dream. I could hardly believe they were gone. A dozen times a day I walked to my mother's room to talk to her, and she wasn't there."

Tears gather in her eyes. She is much like me, after all. I cry when I think of my momma, also.

"Perhaps it was good, my being sent to China to discover the history of our family, suggested by the tablet the first time it was brought to us. The trip was so hard, so difficult, so many perils every day, that I had no time to think much of my parents. Just staying alive was challenge enough. China was–dazzling. Huge, and chaotic, and brutal, and exhilarating, and wonderful. It called everything I had in me, and I discovered more than I could have dreamed I had. I discovered that my ancestor Pan Fulong had founded a prosperous shipping empire, and left it in charge of a cruel cousin until he–or his heir–returned. When I appeared, the cruel side of the family–Black Pans, they are called–gave me a choice. Merge the two lines by marriage, or disappear. My intended mate tried to force himself upon me, at knife point. I resisted, we struggled. He slipped and impaled himself on his knife."

I gasp. Even I have not killed. Yet. The radiant cripple continues to peel *mamey*, missing not a move. I see that killing is not new to her.

"So I fled. The older brother followed me to Manila. I saw his great junk, with the vermillion phoenix flag, enter the harbor as I left aboard a galleon bound for Veracruz. We think some day he will find me here."

"And what happens, then?" I ask.

She stares into my eyes. "I do not know." There is no fear in her eyes, strangely.

"Meanwhile–there is the old treasure, from my countrymen three hundred years ago. I know I can find the secret in the shells that will lead us to it."

The radiant cripple turns to me. "You see, Tabitha. Remember our talk, last night? Your loss of your mother is recent. You cannot imagine anything beyond revenge on the Commandante. But there can be more. There will be more."

She speaks softly, but still her words hurt. I do not want more than revenge. It will be enough. What else could there be?

She senses my defiance. And laughs.

"So Meilu has her treasure to find, and her family to restore to its rightful prominence. Tabitha has her revenge to inflict. These seem large to you, my young friends. And perhaps they are. But these are not of your heart. And a woman's heart is important to her. You must look to your heart, Tabitha. Meilu. Oh, do not abandon your treasure or your revenge. But do not neglect your heart, for that is where your whole life is lived, after treasures and revenge."

I do not understand what she says. What is this talk of heart? "Do you mean–our lives with the *orisha*?" I ask her.

"Partly, it is that. Mostly, though, it has to do with growing up. Becoming a woman."

The China girl looks up, quickly. "What do you mean–becoming a woman?" she asks.

"It is a magical transformation, going from a girl to becoming a woman," the radiant cripple explains. "It is growing into who you truly are."

"And how does it occur?" the strange-eyed girl persists.

The radiant cripple smiles. She cuts the peeled *mamey colorado* in two, and puts a half in front of the two of us. We eagerly eat.

"How do you become a woman?" she repeats. "In the Yoruba culture, we say it is a like a caterpillar spinning its chrysalis and then emerging as a butterfly. You are transformed, utterly. Into something you cannot even imagine as you enter your chrysalis."

"But surely, you can prepare. You can...choose a direction," says the China girl. "Learn from your mother."

The radiant cripple laughs. "We would like to think so. But my experience, and that of my people, is that the caterpillar is meant to eat and grow. When it is ready, it spins the chrysalis. It knows nothing else. It has no idea what kind of butterfly will emerge. Or even if a butterfly will emerge. But always–out of the chrysalis, a butterfly emerges. Sometimes plain, but usually dazzling."

"But ... surely a mother would help her daughter with the process."

Finally the radiant cripple puts down her knife. She speaks carefully. "Yes, you would think so. My experience and that of my people is this. It is good to have a mother to hold you, when you are confused. It is good to have a mother on whose breast you can cry, when you are frightened of the transformation, not knowing what is going on within you. But you must spin your chrysalis by yourself. You must enter it by yourself. And within the chrysalis, you transform. *You* transform. It doesn't matter who or what your mother is, really. Or even that she is there to help you. *You* transform. And a butterfly emerges, and flies off to live its fate."

The strange-eyed girl doesn't like the radiant cripple's words. She stares at the table, breathing hard. "But surely–" she begins, then stops. A deep breath. "The butterfly that emerges," she says. "Surely you have some influence over what you transform into. Or is it all just fate?"

"Partly fate," the radiant cripple answers in a soft voice. "The circumstances that fate thrusts upon you. But partly, yes, your own strength and courage and goodness with which you wrestle with that fate–these contribute also to the woman that emerges."

Her words are difficult to understand. She picks up her knife and begins peeling another fruit. The China girl and I puzzle over her words. Each of us has lost her mother recently. We miss our mothers, very badly. I think we both believe that if our mothers were with us, we would be less confused. Less frightened. But is that true?

It is too much to think about. I sigh. "For me, I leave it to the *orisha*. All is in their hands."

The radiant cripple nods. On that, at least, we agree.

"What are these...*orisha*?" the China girl asks. "Something to do with the bowl of water with the flower in it?" she guesses.

"The *orisha* are the saints of the unseen world," the radiant cripple answers. "We Yoruba can contact them, and receive comfort and strength from them. They take up residence in water decorated with flowers."

"And what are these saints like?" the strange-eyed girl asks, slipping more *mamey colorado* into the bamboo cage for her cricket.

"Much like us, except much stronger, more pure, depending on the saint," the radiant cripple answers. "For me, with the violence in my life, I have always called on *Chango*, the saint expressed in thunder and lightning, he of red and white."

The China girl turns to me. "Is *Chango* your *orisha*, also?"

I shake my head. "I honor *Chango*. Perhaps I will call on him when I kill the Commandante. But the *orisha* of my mother and father is *Obatala*, the pure one, he of white. His spirit is in this amulet, given me by my mother." I touch the talisman around my neck.

"And you, Meilu. Do your people in China have saints you call upon?" asks the radiant cripple.

"Of course. Although we think of them as the *ch'i* energy of extraordinary people who have lived on earth previously. The strength, the energy of the *ch'i* flowing through them, persists after their death, and we draw on that, by honoring them."

"In our room on the ship, you have an altar. A black-faced woman you burn incense to. Is that your saint?" I ask.

"*Ma Tsu*," she nods. "The goddess of the sea. She lived a thousand years ago, on the coast of China in Fujian. She possessed so much *ch'i* that she saved her father and brothers from a great storm at sea, and performed other miracles. She has the *ch'i* energy of the sea in her, as well as its mystery and beauty. Her temples, I have discovered, number many hundreds along the coast of southern China."

The white-tooth Mandinka has been unloading from the wagon as we talk, and working over a fire. Now he puts steaming plates of food on the table.

I hesitate. But I must know. "Lady Silver. You mention violence in your life. We have told you of our lives. What about yours?"

The radiant cripple laughs. She passes plates heaped with food to us.

"I will tell you my story only if you promise to enjoy this food while I talk. Do you promise?"

We two girls nod, and help ourselves to the plates of manioc topped with sugar, corn smothered with butter, pork slivers on a bed of rice and peppers, more food than I have seen in two months. I try not to hurry.

"Like you, Meilu, I had a privileged and happy upbringing," begins the radiant cripple. "I was the favored daughter of a chief, an *otun*, on the richest island off the coast of Nigeria. My father handled business affairs for the *Oba*, the divine king of the region. My body was whole then, and

I could beat my brothers and any boy I knew in our sports–running, throwing, hunting. I particularly enjoyed dancing. Life was grand, and bright, and our home had constant visitors and rang with laughter."

A brief, wistful smile crossed her face.

"But people can be cruel. A rival chief spread false stories of my father. That he was cheating the *Oba*. The world suddenly changed. One day we were favored by the *orisha*. The next day, the *Oba* turned on us, and sold us to the slave traders. My whole family, in a day, was dragged from our beautiful home, put in chains, and marched to a Spanish ship off the island. In an hour our home was fading into the distance. I never again saw my mother, father, or brothers. I suppose they were on the same ship, but so were a thousand others. Nearly half of us died on the voyage. I was not obedient to the slavers, constantly causing trouble. So they chained me apart, in the compartment with the ballast weights. In a storm, the ballast barrels broke loose, and came rolling across the decking toward me. The barrels slammed into me, pinning me against the side of the ship. My hips and legs were crushed. From that night to now, I have never felt or used them again."

I am not eating, now. The food is suddenly unimportant. Though she talks of such terrible things, her face is calm. I wonder, that she does not burn with hatred and desire for revenge.

"They stopped feeding me, knowing I would bring no profit to them, then. Fortunately, we were but days from the first stop, the fortress city of Cartagena on the Spanish Main. An innkeeper saw me as he was buying slaves, or rather saw my arms, which still had muscle on them. He needed someone to pour rum all day and night at his bar, and thought perhaps my arms could do that, even if my legs could do nothing. And I was cheap.

"So I poured rum for sailors, mainly Spaniards, for five years. They could not use me, to satisfy their lust. But they could joke about me, make coarse remarks about my useless hips and legs. Five years, of cruel jokes and pouring rum."

"Then one day the pirates came, and put the town to the sword. It made me happy, to see the *orisha* finally punishing those who had treated me so badly. And I was doubly happy, then, to see Mr. Silver again. He was a ghost from my past, a past I had thought was completely dead and vanished. He suddenly appeared, splashed red with Spanish blood, and carried me away to be his wife. The *orisha* must love to make such jokes."

"You knew the one-legged one, from Nigeria?" I whisper, in shock.

She nods. "Oh yes. Though he was not a cripple, then, nor when he rescued me in Cartagena."

"But–how? Why?"

She laughs. By *Obatala*, I cannot believe she has any laughter in her. After all she has lost. After what she has lived through.

"Only Mr. Silver can choose to tell his story, and he tells it to very few. I will not presume on his right. What I will say is that he is my man, and I am blessed by the *orisha* to have such a man. I will say that we are happy, today, and hope to be happy tomorrow, and that this is enough for us."

So saying, she pushes her plate away, and reaches for another *mamey colorado* to peel.

"But–I don't understand. How you can be so…so happy?" the China girl asks. "You have lost so much. Suffered so much."

"Oh, but I have much reason to be happy," the radiant cripple replies. "I have a good man who loves me. I have strong arms. I have more than enough food to keep me healthy. I have the sweet fruit of *mamey colorado* to savor every day! Why should I not be joyously happy?"

"Yet–" I begin.

"There is no 'yet,'" she insists with a smile. "There is only now–now, in a cool *mogote* cave, with platters of food, a cricket singing sweetly, and two young girls that I like very much. There is nothing but this, and this is good."

I stare at her. She is not lying. This is real for her. More real than the horrors of her past. I wonder. Is it wrong to keep the horrors of the past alive? To keep my hatred of the Commandante burning so fiercely?

No. I cannot give that up. I will have my revenge. But maybe it is not so wrong to enjoy this moment. I tremble, as I look around me. I see things with fresh eyes. Yes. It is cool here. The cricket sings sweetly. The China girl could be a friend. The radiant cripple could be a friend. One day I will have killed the Commandante. What then? Can I have friends, then? Can I laugh, then? Can I spin a chrysalis, enter its strange darkness, and emerge on the other side as my true self? Is that what she meant about a woman's heart?

"*Ha-va-na. Ha-va-na.*" The song drifts from the bamboo cage.

I cut a small piece of the red fruit with a knife, and tentatively push it into the cage. The China girl is staring at me. I return her look. Her eyes are bright, dark as mine. Much like mine.

There is a commotion at the entrance to the cave. The one-legged man and the boy are approaching.

"Rum, Isaiah! Bring me rum!" the one-legged man is roaring. He and the boy are laughing. "And what be the chances that these here ladies have left us any of the pork, Hawkins, me boy? I've a mind we'll be eating nought but manioc, if I knows my lady and those two girls!"

Chapter Ten. Jim Solves the Shells' Secret

Long John and I had a merry lunch with the ladies in the cave, after which we all returned to Long John's home. The others retired to their afternoon naps, a habit which, though Spanish, seemed eminently sensible in a tropical clime, so different than the West Devon coast of England. I remained at the big dining room table, idly playing with the Seven Board pieces given to me by Meilu.

Soon enough I noticed the four cone shells on the other end of the table, whence Long John had carried them from the *Pieces of Eight* the night before. Long John and his past was one mystery that intrigued me more and more. The cone shells were another. I reached across the table and dragged them before me. Tiring of staring at them, I began to touch and move them, and soon found myself, out of recent habit, arranging them as if they were Seven Board pieces. All in a row, first, then changing the order. Every other one upside down, in various orders. But that seemed dull and lacking in imagination.

I began to move the shells into fantastic arrangements, half wondering if I could turn them into a drunken sailor or a soaring eagle. Though no sailors or birds appeared, I continued playing with them. I put all their long tapered ends together in the center, the spires radiating out to the four compass points. Nothing there. I played with the other arrangement, the four spires together in the center, with the tapered ends radiating out. Interesting. The thicker spires, joined together in the center, quite fit together without appreciable space between them, forming a solid mass of the four spires.

It was then I noticed that some of the spires' meandering golden lines were darker and bolder than the rest. And that these bolder lines occupied roughly analogous positions on the four conjoined spires. They didn't quite line up with each other to form a continuous line amongst the four, but were close to it. My hands began to tremble as I switched the positions of the shells, flipping the north-pointing one with the south-pointing. No, not quite. I flipped the east and west ones. Close. Exchanged north with west.

My heart and breath stopped at the same moment. The bolder line running through the four conjoined spires was continuous from one spire to the next. And not only did it form a continuous running line, but the joined line of the four shells looked familiar.

My hair rose on my neck. What was that shape? I had seen it before. It was...It was...

"Long John! Long John!" My shouts echoed through the silent house. I heard stirrings. "Long John!! Long John!!"

Meilu got there first, then Tabitha, both of whom thought I had gone quite crazy, from the wild looks on their faces. Long John soon hobbled into the room, still fastening his belt about his britches as he struggled with his crutch.

"Yes! Yes! Of course!" It was Meilu, predictably, who had seen my arrangement of the cone shells, and the clear outline that had emerged from the bolder lines of all four spires conjoined together. "You are playing like a Chinese, Jim Hawkins!"

"What the devil are ye talking about?" demanded Long John.

I found it difficult to speak. My head was spinning. My heart had fortunately resumed its beating, but now was threatening to quite burst from my chest.

"The cone shells, Long John," I finally stammered. "When they're like this, the lines on the spires form–" I pointed to it. "Form that outline!"

Long John peered over at the shells. "Why, that they do. An outline sort of thing, by thunder. But what the devil is the outline, Jim? It don't mean a thing to me."

"Don't you see it, Long John? It's the outline of a bay. It's a bay I learned from the charts back in my room at the Admiral Benbow. It's clearly the bay we sailed into two days ago–Havana Bay!"

"By the powers!" roared Long John as he bent over the shells. "Shiver me timbers if it's not! There be the long mouth, there the bulge where the city sits, there Atares inlet–it's Havana Bay! Jim, ye've solved the riddle of the shells!" His eyes were bulging, his breath ragged.

"Rum!" Long John roared. "Bring us rum. We've some celebrating to do!"

Soon servants were scurrying into the room, tankards of rum on trays.

It was Meilu who broke the spell. "But Long John. Jim. So it's Havana Bay. It's a very large bay. Do we know where the treasure is within this very large bay?"

That stopped us all short. Four heads simultaneously bent to the shells. Tabitha spotted it first. Her thin black finger appeared on the coast just east of the mouth of the bay.

"There. A short line thrusts through the coastline. It spoils the outline. It must indicate the presence of something."

Long John paused, a tankard of rum halfway to his mouth. I had never before seen Long John pause mid-way through a drink of rum. It staggered me.

He bent over. "Aye, it be an intersection. None others of these along the coast or in the bay itself, I presumes?"

We all looked closely. No. It was a perfect coastline, with only one intersecting line–the line passing through it perpendicularly where Tabitha had indicated.

"By the powers, that be pointing right at where the Del Morro castle sits today," Long John whispered. "Right at."

"They built the castle over the treasure?" Meilu asked with a groan. "Then it's lost to us."

"No! Think!" I interrupted. "This is treasure from six ships. They wouldn't have buried it like Flint did his gold. That's too big a hole to dig."

"Lunch," Tabitha said quietly. "Where we ate lunch yesterday."

We all looked up at her as if she had lost her senses.

"Lunch? What do ham, *mamey colorado*, and tea have to do with this?" I snapped.

"No, *where* we had lunch," Tabitha spit back at me.

"Of course! A cave!" Meilu said.

"There's no cave under Del Morro Castle," Long John said. "Lots of dungeons, I hear–" he shivered. "But no cave."

"Look at the line," said Tabitha. "It goes from the sea side of the coast. It passes *into* the land side. Why not a *sea cave*? Open only at low tide, in the cliff the castle sits atop?"

We all grew wide-eyed.

"Ye be claiming, my friend, that a sea cave sits *under* Del Morro Castle?" whispered Long John. "A sea cave ye get to by boat at low tide, that be bulging with Chinee treasure?"

Tabitha shrugged her shoulders.

"Rum all around!" Long John said in a suddenly booming voice. "And pack your things, me friends. I feel a sudden hankering to be back on the *Pieces of Eight*, and making a leisurely sail to Havana Bay, arriving at the entrance about sunset or thereabouts. Anyone care to jine me?"

We all grabbed a glass of rum, and clinked our glasses in a toast.

"Treasure!" we shouted with one voice.

Tabitha broke the excited silence as we gulped the rum down and savored the warm tingle in our throats.

"Rum is a gift from the *orisha*. I think I like it."

Chapter Eleven. Meilu Visits her Ancestors

My Seven Board was of a sudden quite popular among the barbarians on the sea voyage back to Havana Bay that day. The boy Hawkins' use of its method to solve the riddle of the cone shells made everyone curious about it. Even the slave girl Tabitha, in spite of her grief, and the dark desire for revenge which consumed her, was attracted to the ancient game. The two of them spent the afternoon hunched over the pieces on the deck, eagerly trading turns and challenging each other to make this or that fantastic figure. I cannot doubt that my countryman Zhou Wen three hundred years ago had the Seven Board in mind when he so carefully had his craftsmen insert his own marks on the wandering lines of the spires of the cone shells.

I will admit that I had expected to be the one to solve the riddle, and the barbarian boy's triumph sat ill with me. Yet I had already noted his quickness, and the supple way his mind worked, so that my disappointment did not spoil the day. Indeed, I was glad to have such a quick mind in the company as we sought the long-lost treasures from my ancestral homeland. The north coast of Cuba passed by us quickly and agreeably through the afternoon of sailing, palm-lined beaches studded with occasional lagoons. I sat with my back comfortably against the apple barrel, whistling an accompaniment to the melodious "*Ha-va-na*" of my cricket.

Soon the La Punta Castle was on our starboard, occupying the west side of the mouth of Havana Bay. The much more massive Del Morro Castle loomed atop the high bluff on the other, east side of the mouth of the Bay, in front of us. I knew we all secretly despaired at the thought of Zhou Wen's treasure resting directly beneath the imposing fortress. The castle's two levels of ramparts teemed with soldiers watching the harbor and the sea. Cannon lined the walls, including the giant "Twelve Apostles" aimed directly into the mouth of the bay from the lower rampart.

"Take heart, me lads and lasses," Long John said, sensing our mood as we sailed past the bay's mouth. "All those men and guns be concentrated on ships in the harbor and far out to sea. Why, they can't even rightly see anything at the base of the cliff on the seaward side."

We eagerly trained our eyes on the base of the cliff, which abruptly rose from the sea some two hundred feet, atop which the Del Morro Castle sat. I sent a silent prayer to *Ma Tsu*, to reveal to us the mystery gathered somewhere alongside her sea's juncture with the cliff.

"The charts say the sea be very deep on the cliff side there," Silver commented. "No doubt that cliff plunges down another several hundred feet, I wager." He turned to the first mate at the wheel of *Pieces of Eight*. "Where be the tide, Isaiah?"

"Hit low an hour ago, Cap'n," the youth replied. "Beginning to rise, now."

"Not perfect, but we'll see if there's anything left of any opening. If sich there be," he added skeptically. "Take us as close by as you can safely manage, me lad," he instructed Isaiah.

The sun was dipping into the sea behind us as we passed along the base of the cliff, casting a warm golden glow on the soaring cliff face. Tabitha's keen eyes were the first to spot it.

"There! Directly under the jutting rock!"

"Where? Where?" we all cried, not another eye finding it.

"Rising six feet above waterline," she answered. "An opening, wider at the bottom, just wide enough for a longboat. Under that square jutting rock."

"Aye, I sees it, too," yelled Silver. "And I'll wager that pecu'lar square rock weren't there four hundred years ago. It looks too tidy for me eyes."

Soon it was apparent to all of us. We stared, awestruck, as the *Pieces of Eight* sailed by the spot.

The boy voiced all our thoughts.

"It's too narrow for a boat," he said, his voice crestfallen. "It's not but five feet wide or so at waterline."

"True enough, Hawkins," I agreed. "But see how the opening broadens at its base. At low tide, when the waterline is two feet lower, the opening will be wider, wider by perhaps three feet or so. Plenty wide enough for a longboat."

"Aye, so long as you pull your oars in," Silver said. "I think she's right, me hearties." He turned to Isaiah again. "Take us twenty minutes up the coast, lad, then swing 'er around, and back here. It'll be dark by then. We'll put to some hundred feet offshore, launch the longboat, and sneak up to the cave's entrance in darkness, hidden from all those eyes on the castle ramparts."

He looked down the row of us, glued to the bulwarks, eyes riveted on the opening in the cliff. "Assuming there's any aboard this here ship that hankers to do a bit of exploring tonight."

Three pairs of eyes swung to him, and as many chins eagerly nodded assent.

"Aye, I figured as much," the one-legged barbarian said with a grin.

* * * * *

An hour later the *Pieces of Eight* sat becalmed, with sails rolled, in the darkness at the base of the cliff. Del Morro Castle loomed grey above us. The moon was new, so the darkness was nearly complete, modified only by the dim light from the castle's lighthouse above, and the stars much farther above. Silver had the starboard longboat lowered into the water, so that the *Pieces of Eight* hid its launch from any sharp night-eyes in the castle. Silently we climbed down the starboard ladder and dropped into the boat. I once again uttered a silent prayer to *Ma Tsu*. We were entering her realm, the restless sea.

"I don't like this, Long John," the boy was saying. "The Commandante's bound to be curious why the *Pieces of Eight* anchored here overnight. The longboat may be invisible, but the ship isn't."

"Aye, and when he asks, I'll just say we arrived at the mouth of the bay after his soldiers pulled the bloody chain up across the entrance, which they do every sunset," Silver replied. "You mind that chain, do ya not, boy? It stretches from the La Punta Castle on the west across the narrow mouth, and be spooled up or down in the water by gears at the base of Del Morro Castle to the east, on that lower rampart. The chain's pulled tight and up to the surface at night. Makes 'em feel secure in the darkness, keeping bad eggs like us'n from sneaking into their harbor." He smothered a chuckle.

The oars were wrapped in cloth, which kept them silent but made them heavier and more difficult to pull. Silver was on one, the boy on the other. The boy tired quickly, and Tabitha rudely pushed him aside and took over the rowing from him. Though no older than the boy and myself, and as slim, she was sleekly muscled, and evidently impervious to fatigue.

We arrived at the cliff face. In the dark, the opening was invisible to us. The others were very nervous, breathing in jagged breathes as the waves pushed us against the cliff face. I was on *Ma Tsu's* sea, and I trusted her to look after us, so long as we showed respect to her and kept our wits about us.

"Row along the face," I whispered. "I'll jab the spare oar against it until we find the opening." So we crab-walked along the face of the cliff, the muffled oars dripping water, my oar scraping softly along the rock. Soon the oar was scraping air.

"Here!"

Right next to it, we could finally see the opening, a deeper darkness than the cliff surrounding it. We maneuvered the longboat around, and pulled in the oars. Hawkins, in front now, grabbed either side of the opening with his hands, and pulled us into the cave.

Indeed it was narrow. The sides of the longboat scraped against the rock to either side. Soon we were stuck, wedged against each side of the narrow cave.

"Push the boat lower in the water, where it's wider," Silver suggested. Since we were in the opening fully now, we all four of us pushed down against the walls enclosing us, and as the boat sunk dangerously close to the waterline, we broke free, and were able to shove ourselves further into the entrance.

Soon we were stuck again. Try as we might, we couldn't shove the boat any lower. Water was lapping over the edges. We were hot, and sweating from our exertion, and the cave seemed to be getting narrower. A feeling of being trapped and smothered crept over me in the utter blackness. The sea was *Ma Tsu's*. This dark, narrowing cave belonged to some other spirit. Rather than an opening into a larger cavern, the cave seemed to be a dead end that would drown us all.

"Long John!" came the voice of Hawkins, in the front of the boat. "The walls disappear but a foot ahead! The cave opens up!"

"Lay to it with heart, my friends," Long John urged in a hoarse voice. "One more shove down and forward, and we'll burst free of this here infernal prison."

We shoved, the boat very nearly going underwater, and suddenly we popped through the embrace of the walls. The boat spurted into–what? More darkness, but at least there were no walls of rock hemming us in.

"Lanterns, me lads and lasses," hissed Silver.

We groped for the canvas bags containing the four lanterns on the floor of the boat, floating in several inches of water, and secured one each. I struck the tinder that I'd kept dry in my sleeve, and passed the light around. The light from four glowing lanterns seemed unbearable, and momentarily blinded us. Slowly our eyes adjusted, and we held the lanterns aloft and gazed around us, in wide-eyed wonder.

The cavern was large, about the size of Silver's *Pieces of Eight*. Row after row of lacquer chests were stacked on the wide rocky ledges to either side of our tongue of water, the topmost chest of each stack opened to reveal the contents. Here were chests of ivory and jade carvings–mythical animals, mountain scenes, flowers, and the round *pi* discs. Over there were chests of the finest porcelain–flower vases, thin-walled plates, cups, and bowls decorated with brilliant gold and green and vermilion. And over there were chests brimming with silk, which overflowed the chests and streamed down nearly to the floor, shimmering bolts of brilliant cloth embroidered with the finest stitchings of cranes and dragons and mountains. Hundreds upon hundreds of chests, chests as far as the eye could see, their contents glimmering in the lantern light.

And in the middle of everything, making me feel at home, a huge teak altar to *Ma Tsu*, goddess of the sea. She sat, larger than life-size, regal on a jade throne with the customary strings of pearl adorning her forehead, her black face and mother-of-pearl eyes gleaming in the flickering light. The table before her was covered with the choicest silk, jade, and porcelain, and a large flask of what appeared to be solid gold, gleaming dully. Overcome with awe, I bowed my head to the goddess, and thanked her for bringing me and my friends here to her, after three hundred years of solitude.

For the second time since I had known him, Silver was speechless. We sat in the boat, casting our lantern light about in stunned silence. It was the boy, Hawkins, who finally spoke, his voice soft with awe.

"I thought Flint's gold in Ben Gunn's cave was beautiful. But this–why, this treasure is...is *things* of beauty. Treasure made beautiful, by human minds and hands."

"Aye, Jim Hawkins," breathed Silver softly, finally finding his tongue. "This puts Flint's gold and silver to shame, it does." He swallowed hard. "Meaning no disrespect to silver and gold, of course," he hastily added. "And mindful that these beautiful things will bring a powerful lot of gold into our hands."

Silver stood, and held his lantern high to better see the treasure. "A powerful amount of gold! Do you a mind, boy, how much all that silk alone will bring?" He was shouting now, his voice bouncing off the walls. "Not to mention the China porcelain. No one but your Squire and Kings and Queens can afford porcelain from China. Now we've got a whole shipload of it. It's all ours!" To our surprise, he began to dance a happy little one-legged jig in the boat.

I didn't even know a jig could be danced with one leg–but there it was, rocking the boat alarmingly.

"Meilu," asked Tabitha, as we grabbed the sides of the boat to steady it, and Hawkins pushed Silver back to his seat. "The black-faced one on the altar. That is–?"

It was the first time she had used my name, I realized.

"Yes. *Ma Tsu*, Queen of Heaven," I replied. "The goddess of the sea. Every one of Admiral Zhou Wen's ships had an altar to her."

"She looks almost happy," observed Hawkins. "Not at all fierce or angry, the way the sea often is."

"We Chinese believe the sea, and mountains and valleys, are charged with *ch'i* energy, which flows in a path called the *Tao*," I said, making soft echoes in the far reaches of the cavern. "Sometimes the flow is violent and dangerous. Sometimes gentle and smooth. But never evil or malevolent. That comes only from humans, not from the sea or the mountains. We study the flow of the *Tao* and respect it, so we can use it to our advantage–play with it, almost."

"Aye, that be right int'resting, I'm sure," Silver's voice broke in. "And it be right pleasing to sit and enjoy the sight of all this treasure. But what I've a mind of just now be this here rising tide, and the tight squeeze we had getting in here just minutes ago."

We all reluctantly agreed. Silver and Hawkins used their tricorners to bail water from the boat, as Tabitha and I paddled back to the entrance. I cast a backward look at *Ma Tsu*, serene on her jade throne, surrounded by the treasures of our race. At the cave entrance, to our great dismay, the rising tide had shrunk the opening considerably. The boat could in no way pass out.

"Trapped, by the powers!" announced Silver, a note of panic in his voice. "No food, only an hour's oil in the lanterns, and we're trapped!" He glanced about frantically, slapping the side of the boat in frustration. An ominous echo bounced from wall to wall.

"Nonsense," I replied. "We'll simply leave the boat here, and swim back to the ship." Tabitha shrugged, and nodded her assent. Silver and the boy raised horrified faces to me.

"You *can* swim, can't you?" I asked.

They sheepishly shook their heads.

Tabitha and I rolled our eyes.

"Come. While there's still an opening at all," Tabitha said, standing up. "We'll flip the longboat over. It may pass through upside down, when the boat is widest at the bottom, rather than the top. Our two pirates hold onto the side of the boat. The lanterns and oars go on top, on the flat keel. Meilu and I pull the boat through the opening. When on the other side, we right the boat. And let the two pirates take command again."

It was the longest I had ever heard her speak.

So saying, and without waiting for the approval of the two cowering men, Tabitha jumped out of the boat into the water, and began to pull her side of the boat down. Amidst howls and curses from Silver and the boy, I joined her, finding the water agreeably cool. With a mighty shout the two men hit the water, flailing about, as the longboat overturned. Tabitha and I each grabbed one of the men by the collar, and held them up while they slapped white-knuckled grips onto the boat. Silver was swearing mightily, his vocabulary far outstripping my knowledge of English.

Tabitha slung the four extinguished lanterns and the oars atop the keel, along with Silver's battered old crutch of what he claimed was English oak. With our two mighty pirates securely attached to the boat, we girls swam to the front, grabbed hold of the bowline, and began towing our load to the cave entrance.

The small opening was filled with the echoes of Tabitha and I grunting as we pulled the boat seaward, not to mention the frightened howlings of the two men. Soon Tabitha and I burst into laughter, so comical was the fright of the men. Laughing, grunting with exertion, kicking our legs hard underwater, we finally burst out of the sea cave.

It was like emerging into another world. Above us, the stars shone like small bursts of fire, numberless in the heavens. After the confines of the sea cave, the air smelled gloriously fresh, and we gulped in huge lungfulls of it. I caught Tabitha's eyes–she too felt it, like me. A sudden rush of joy, of keen happiness just to be alive, to be laughing and amongst friends, muscles pleasantly tired, the sharp taste of seawater in our mouths. We whooped and laughed and splashed water at each other and the two men. We had found a staggering treasure, the night was precious, and we were immersed in *Ma Tsu's* sea!

The men quickly tired of our celebrations, and begged us to right the longboat. Righting it was more difficult than capsizing it, but the four of us at length succeeded, and pitched the lanterns, oars, and crutch into it. Hawkins eagerly slithered into the boat like an eel. Silver was another story. Hawkins pulled on him from above, in the boat, while Tabitha and I pushed with all our strength from below, in the water, all of us fueled by more laughter. Finally he tumbled into the boat, oaths scattering in all directions. Immediately he was up, his crutch under his left arm, and dancing his one-legged jig again.

"Treasure, me lads and lasses! More treasure than I've ever seen in me long wicked life! Chinee treasure, at that. *Yo ho ho and a bottle of rum*!"

In his happiness he drew his sword and began waving it about as he bellowed his pirate song to the heavens.

Tabitha was about to pull herself into the boat. I laid my hand on her arm, to stop her.

"Sister. Wait until the staggering old pirate has sheathed his sword."

She laughed, and nodded. Then our eyes quickly met, as we both realized what I had called her. The stars glittered, on fire, and Silver sang, drunk on treasure, as we two sisters enjoyed the coolness of the embracing sea.

* * * *

She stared into the returned blackness of the cave. Three hundred years of dark and quiet had been shattered by the strange visitors. One of them was her race. The others–strange beings! She sat, exploring the currents of ch'i introduced by the visitors. One bold, but painfully tempered, smoothed by the agonizing roughness of experience. The others turbulent, confused, exuberant, hesitant, rushing into the future but frightened and unsure of the transformation awaiting them. A surge of pity, and amusement, whirled into the vast river of her own ch'i. Would they return? The island was awash with strong flows of cruelty and hatreds. And something approached from afar, unknown to the visitors, but entwined intimately with them, about to break over them as a storm. Would they live to return? She leaned that direction ever so slightly, shifting the inertia of her own massive ch'i to make it more likely. Not guaranteed–even a saint of three thousand years could not just decree anything! But more likely, yes. It amused her to make it more likely. To play with the ch'i and render the wondrous world even more strange and startling than it tended to. A pulse trembled on the surface of the water in the cave, and began a slow, majestic journey through the narrow opening, shifting things as it traveled.

Chapter Twelve. Tankas and Giants

Ma *Tsu's* pearl-draped forehead glittered in my dreams all that night aboard the *Pieces of Eight*. We all gathered at the railing on deck early the next morning, and basked in the warmth of the low sun as the *Pieces of Eight* sailed toward the entrance to Havana Bay. Without saying anything, each of us uneasily eyed the imposing fortress atop the cliff just above our sea cave. Finding the treasure turned out to be the easy part. Getting it out of the sea cave from under the very nose of the Spaniards–now that was going to be difficult.

We watched as the great chain stretching across the narrow mouth of the bay in front of us was slowly unspooled from its wheel on the lower rampart of Del Morro Castle, monstrous gear spokes slowly meshing with the great capstan pushed in a circle by a dozen brawny soldiers. As the gear shaft revolved, and more and more of the chain fell free of the wheel, it sank deeply enough into the water so that even the great galleons could pass over it unencumbered.

I saw the ship just as we sailed over the chain, sitting at anchor dark and square and ominous in the middle of the bay, the soaring phoenixes fluttering atop the middle mast. A sharp cry escaped me as I swayed, dizzy with fear.

"What is it?" Tabitha asked at my elbow, seeing the stiffness that suddenly ruled my limbs.

"The Black Pans," I whispered, more to myself than to her. "They arrived while we were at Vinales Valley. Grandfather!" There was no time for explanations. The Black Pans could be at our home even now. I kicked off my shoes, and dropped my shawl on deck. Climbing onto the railing, I dove into the water far below. I hit the water hard, and it swirled cold and biting around me, but immediately I set off with strong strokes for the docks. Behind me, I could vaguely hear my friends calling. I had no time for friends, or treasure. Only Grandfather mattered, and the mahogany tablet of Pan Fulong sitting at the back of our ancestor altar.

In ten minutes I pulled myself onto the docks, and set off running through the Plaza de Armas and down Calle Obispo. In another ten minutes I arrived at our home. Inside the door, Hatuey lay on the tiles of the entry courtyard, a pistol in his outstretched hand. He was cold, a knife sticking from his chest. I stumbled through the house, dreading what I would find. Grandfather's room was empty, though in shambles, books and chairs scattered about. The same in the central courtyard. I did not want to think what I might find in the reception hall, but forced my trembling legs to take me there through the arched door. The floor was mercifully empty of any body, but the doors of the ancestor altar were wide open. Spirit tablets lay upended within the altar. And at the very back–nothing but an empty space.

The Black Pans had Pan Fulong's tablet. And they had Grandfather as well.

It was too much for me. I slumped to the floor before the altar, and cried. Cried for Grandfather in the clutches of the cruel older brother. Cried for my mother and father, snatched away by the Spanish disease. For Hatuey, stretched cold on the tiles of the courtyard. Cried for my loneliness. For my confusion. Cried for everything.

Tabitha's voice floated to me from far away. I didn't know what to make of it. Soon she was beside me, holding me. I heard the voice of Hawkins. Then Isaiah. Taino.

Tabitha helped me to a chair. I sat, bewildered by grief. She was brushing my tears away, brushing my hair out of my face. Talking softly to me. Like a sister.

Lastly, the thump of Silver's wooden leg entering. "What in thunder?"

"Quiet!" Tabitha hissed at him. "Let her be!"

I breathed deep. "It's all right. I–I can think."

"Who did this, Meilu?" asked Hawkins.

A deep breathe. I tried to talk, but couldn't.

Tabitha, softly. "You said something about Black Pans, before you took off. From China? That you mentioned in the *mogote* cave to Lady Silver and me?"

I nodded. Another deep breathe. I glanced at Hawkins and Silver. "In China, I discovered another branch of our family. A twisted branch, the Black Pans. They must yield their control of our family shipping empire when the White Pans return."

"Ah," muttered Hawkins, ever the sharp one. "And you, and your ancestor from three hundred years ago–the White Pans."

Another nod. "In China, Shanghai, the Black Pans gave me a choice–marry the younger son of the Blacks, or die. I struggled with the younger son, and he slipped and impaled himself on his knife. I fled, as he lay bleeding to death."

Silence, as Hawkins and Silver and the others absorbed it. Tabitha pieced it together first. "So–one of the Blacks has followed you here. For revenge."

"Revenge, yes. But mainly to claim the spirit tablet of Pan Fulong." I motioned toward the ransacked altar. "They have it, now. And Grandfather." I tried to stand up. And promptly collapsed back into the chair, Tabitha's arms keeping me upright.

"I must go save Grandfather. To their junk." I tried to stand. And fell down again.

"Methinks this calls for some thinking, me dearie," said Silver softly. "You and Tabitha just sit there, and collect yourselves," he went on. "Jim, boy, you and Isaiah visit the kitchen, see if you can make some hot tea and grub for us'n." He turned to the Indian. "Taino. Get that knife out of your kinsman's chest, and cover him up with something. I reckon you know how to bury him proper-like, according to your people?"

The Indian nodded gravely, and glided off.

An hour later, I felt better. I could even stand without falling over. My friends were gathered around the sandalwood table. I had cleaned up the altar behind us, righting the remaining tablets, and lit incense before the remaining ancestors, and *Ma Tsu* beside them. Hawkins and Isaiah had cleared away the remains of a fortifying meal.

"Thank you," I said to all. "Now I must go to the junk, and rescue Grandfather."

"Not alone, you're not," asserted Tabitha, to nods all around.

"This is not your concern," I said. "It is bigger than you. It is three hundred years old, and stretches all the way to Shanghai. You aren't involved."

"We begs to differ, young lady," Silver said with a grin. "When we rescued Tabitha, her'n the Commandante's bad blood became our bad blood. You threw in your lot with us to solve Billy Bone's old shells, and that makes you one o' us. We're sharing all that treasure in your black-faced lady's sea cave below Del Morro, and by thunder we'll share in your troubles with whatever outlaw Pans you got, be they black, blue, or red."

Even I had to join the laughter at the old pirate's words. They may be barbarians, but they are decent people. Who was I to question the universe, if the universe had given them to me to help fight the Black Pans? The question, of course, remained. Just how did I and my peculiar friends rescue Grandfather and defeat the Black Pans?

* * * * *

Silver had anchored the *Pieces of Eight* some two hundred yards west of the Black Pans' oceangoing junk, so they looked into the late afternoon sun in our direction. We felt safe standing at the railings and examining the vessel and its inhabitants.

"Grandfather will be alive," I mused. "They will use him as bait to lure me."

"And if he's as sharp as I remember, he'll be trying to let us know where he is," Hawkins added. "So we look for–what?"

"Cigar smoke," I said with a soft laugh. "The sure sign of Grandfather."

"I've seen many a strange varmint in me life," Silver drawled from behind his telescope. "But I never seen creatures as mis-shaped as those manning that junk."

He passed the telescope to me. I lofted it, and focused.

"Tanka!" I whispered. The crew were all Tanka!

"What?" asked Tabitha.

"Water folk," I answered. "Vermin, my tutor in Shanghai also called them."

"That fits," Silver observed. "Do ya mind those flat foreheads? The long arms? It be un-nervin'. They just don't look right," he concluded.

"What are you talking about?" Hawkins asked crossly.

I handed the telescope back to Silver. "The crew. They're a foreign race. Not Chinese at all. They're said to be from Southeast Asia, perhaps Annam, perhaps Malaya. Where Pan Fulong originally founded his trading empire, in fact. In China, they're restricted to their boats, not allowed to live on land with us Chinese."

"How do they earn their living, restricted to boats?" asked Tabitha.

"The men, fisherfolk. The women–sorcerors, and prostitutes," I said, blushing.

"Well, I don't see no womenfolk, mores the pity," observed Silver with a cackle, again behind his telescope. "But those men–they do look pecu'ler."

"There!" shouted the sharp-eyed Tabitha. "The third port hole from the right, below decks. A cigar butt just flew out of it."

"By thunder ye've got the eyes, dearie," said Silver, his telescope trained on the spot. "And there be smoke drifting out o' that port hole, or I'm a vermin Tanka, I am."

"Grandfather," I whispered.

"Well, we've located him," said Hawkins. "Now how do we get him from there?"

Silence.

"Let's figure what we're up against," Silver began. "I've seen half a dozen o' them vermin Tanka. Mayhaps that many again, below decks."

"There. The Older Brother," I whispered. "The tall one, just emerged from the hatch in front of the poop deck."

"Arrogant-looking cuss," said Silver from behind his telescope. "But tall, and strong. Shiver me timbers–look at th' giant *behind* him! The Arab with the beard."

I groaned. Even without the telescope, you could see the man was huge.

"Doubtless his first mate," I guessed. "To keep the Tanka in line."

Silver snapped his telescope shut. "So. A dozen or so vermin sailors, a big captain, and a bigger first mate. That be a rough sityation, dearie."

I couldn't help but nod my agreement. *Ma Tsu–I need your help.*

"I be at your service, you can lay to that," Silver said. "But I can't ask me lads to board that ship in a brawl. It be too dangerous by half, and that's the truth of it."

Another reluctant nod from me. "Beyond that, a fight that lasts any length gives them plenty of time to kill Grandfather before he can be rescued," I added.

"Long John, you've more experience than me in this," began Hawkins. "But my guess on vermin is that loyalty is not their strong suit. What do you think–if we take out the captain and the big Arab, maybe–just maybe–the crew aren't so keen to fight?"

"Hawkins! Of course!" I said, a jolt of hope surging through me. "That sounds just like Tanka. Particularly Tanka under the heavy hand of an Arab and a Black Pan."

"They're expecting you to attempt a rescue of your Grandfather," Hawkins continued. "So let's give them what they expect. They capture us, we're brought before the captain and his Arab. Their guard is down, they think we're just two harmless kids."

"Perhaps they are not so far wrong in that," Tabitha observed drily.

"But suddenly, we hit them with secret weapons!" Hawkins continued.

"What secret weapons, to overpower this captain and his Arab?" pressed Tabitha.

We looked at each other, blank faces staring at blank faces.

Then I pulled out the cloisonne pendant from my tutor in Shanghai. I pressed the ivory ring. When the razor edges had swiveled out, I whirled the deadly star at Silver's main mast, which was thankfully quite broad. The star sank deep into the soft pine wood.

Silver was the first to gain his voice. "By thunder. That be a weapon. It won't take out anything more than one man, and ye can't get it back quickly. But it be a weapon. Ye'd have to sneak–or be taken–might close to the man to use it, though."

Hawkins reached inside his vest, and pulled out his pistol.

"They'll search ye and find that in a second," Silver said. "And ye can't hit a man reliably with it unless you're well nigh right up on him, again."

"I'll hide it in my boot," Hawkins said. "Maybe they won't think to search there."

We all had to laugh as we noticed he was barefoot, as always on *Pieces of Eight.*

"Avast! I'll put boots on. They're in my cabin," he protested.

"Meaning no disrespect, but it'd be might nice to have a backup weapon," said Silver dubiously.

"I am your backup weapon," Tabitha said quietly in the silence that followed. "If you allow yourselves to be captured, you will get close enough to use those weapons," she said. "That will get you by the crew without having to fight them." She paused to think. "While all attention is on your capture, I sneak aboard at the other end of the boat. It is my weapon, my stealth. I will join you, unseen, at some point."

Silver reached into his boot and drew out a knife, battered but sharp of blade.

"This be me very own dirk, dearie," he said to Tabitha. "I'd be might grateful if ye add it to your arsenal–in case it might be helpful."

Tabitha took it, and carefully inserted it under her belt, in the small of her back.

"This old buccaneer be too large and clumsy to be part of this expydition," Silver said. "But I'll be standing by, with me lads, once ye've secured the ship."

I nodded. "Tonight, then. In darkness. I'll pretend to try to sneak up to Grandfather's porthole on the port side, with Hawkins. Be loud enough to be caught. Tabitha sneaks aboard on the starboard side. Tries to follow as best she can, as Hawkins and I are brought to the captain and his Arab."

"And then?" Hawkins asked, hopefully.

"From there, we make it up," I answered. "Use our weapons as we can."

Silence.

"Int'resting plan," Silver observed. "But I can't fathom a better 'un."

"I must do it. For Grandfather. For Pan Fulong," I said. "None of you is required to accompany me."

There was no hesitation. "I'm with you," Tabitha said, quiet but determined. "And me," Hawkins added, firm and clear.

"Methinks we could all use a wee bit o' rum to sharpen our minds afore dark," Silver offered. "That part I can provide."

Chapter Thirteen. Throwing Stars and Pistols

I lit incense before my small shrine to *Ma Tsu* on Silver's ship an hour after sunset, glancing over to the bowl of water near Tabitha's bed. We very clearly needed all the help we could possibly get from Tabitha's *orisha* and my Chinese saint. As smoke from the incense curled past *Ma Tsu's* pearls, I asked her to keep my mind clear and my movements sure. My fate–my family's fate–was in her hands.

The jumpy sensations in my stomach and my mind refused to quiet. I was glad to think of *Ma Tsu* and give my fate to her. But my mind still raced and my stomach rebelled. I felt hot.

I checked the silk bands wrapped around my sleeves and cuffs, to ensure their not impeding my movements. From the little bamboo cage next to the altar came a soft whirring noise, then a bell-like "*Ha-va-na*." I picked the cage up. Giving the cloisonne pendant around my neck a gentle tug, I rose and walked up the stairs to the deck, going slowly to make sure my jerky steps didn't make me trip.

Tabitha and Hawkins were already there, pacing nervously. My sister Tabitha was in black, and nearly invisible, even to me, when she stopped moving and stood staring at me. Hawkins looked strange in his heavy boots below his linen shirt and breeches. But somehow more grown up. His eyes didn't falter when they met mine.

We walked past the apple barrel on the waist, to the gate in the railing, where Silver was standing, looking very nervous also as he leaned into his crutch.

"Here's my favorite cricket," I said as I extended the bamboo cage to him. "Take good care of him if–if I don't return."

Silver began to remonstrate at my words, but I silenced him with my eyes.

"More. If I don't return, take my *Ma Tsu* altar in the stateroom below, to Grandfather's and my home. Light incense at the main altar one last time. Then burn the house, and everything in it. Before the Black Pans can get there. Do this for me."

He took the cricket cage from me, and simply nodded. He said not a word–unusual, for him–but touched his knuckles to his forelock in a salute as we three moved past him and climbed down into the waiting longboat.

Hawkins and I locked the oars, and pulled. When we were halfway to the dark bulk of the Chinese junk, Tabitha slipped quietly into the water, and began swimming to the far side of the junk. Several minutes later, we arrived at the third porthole on the port side. I could smell Grandfather's cigar smoke, and it made me smile, despite the tightness in my throat.

Pulling up to the porthole, I pursed my lips and imitated the sound of my *Ha-va-na* cricket several times. I waited a minute, then repeated the sounds.

"Meilu?" came Grandfather's voice from the porthole.

"Grandfather!" I answered, not so softly. "Are you all right?"

"I don't like the Black Pans," Grandfather answered with a soft laugh. "I don't like the Older Brother, or his Arab first mate. They almost make their strange crew look good. And what in heaven are you doing here?"

"We've come to rescue you," I answered, again rather loudly.

"Quiet, child. They'll hear you."

"That's part of our plan," I whispered back.

A brief silence. "Interesting plan," he said. I didn't much like it when Silver had said the same thing earlier, and it didn't sound any better from my Grandfather.

"Meilu. Don't bother with me. You're the last White Pan–you're the important one."

"I'm going to rescue you. And I'm going to rescue Pan Fulong's spirit tablet," I said stubbornly. "I won't leave without both of you."

"Well, I–"

Two bodies erupted from the water on either side of our longboat at that moment, and long, strong arms grasped our gunwales. In a second, two Tanka had slithered into the boat and held knives at our throats. Our vaunted 'secret weapons' were useless at this close a quarter. Tabitha's words came back to me with force–maybe we were just kids.

Soon two more Tanka were in the water, towing the longboat to the ladder. Hawkins and I were dragged up the ladder–*by my holy Ma Tsu, these Tanka were incredibly strong*–and onto the deck of the junk. The Arab awaited us there. He was even larger than we thought, towering over us by several feet. He seemed very pleased. Without a word he jerked his head, indicating us to follow him.

We passed to the poop deck and down a spacious passage to a burnished teak door.

The Arab pounded on the door.

"*Lai lai*," came a voice from within. Enter.

The Arab stepped back, opened the door, and shoved Hawkins and me into the room. To our left was a large window looking out into the night. To our right, halfway down the room, was a massive desk, burnished teak like the door, with a lantern on it. The lantern illuminated Older Brother, sitting behind the desk. He registered no surprise when he saw us enter and march before the desk. Half a dozen of the Tanka crew slithered in the door behind us and spread against the wall to the right of the door, a few streaming around the corner against the wall behind the desk, out of the flare of light from the lantern. I saw a form in the darkness there that wasn't Tanka, and hope flickered in my heart–my sister was here.

Older Brother's black eyes gleamed. He looked me up and down, as if he were examining an insect or a piece of furniture. The same cold look his younger brother had given me. He glanced quickly at Hawkins, then back at me.

"You are more difficult to deal with than we imagined, dear cousin," he said in a smooth, quiet voice. "Yet here you are, finally. Enjoying, once again, our estimable Black Pan hospitality."

Without taking his burning eyes off me, he said harshly to the Arab, "Search the boy."

Before Hawkins or I had a chance to move, the Arab's huge hands were running down Hawkin's body. They moved without pause to his boots and extracted the pistol. The glimmer of hope that Tabitha's presence in the darkness behind the desk had kindled was snuffed out as the Arab placed the pistol on the desk beside Older Brother's clasped hands there.

"How quaint. How charming," he said with a soft laugh. "A boy with a pistol, your guardian, to protect you and rescue your grandfather. How... *pitiful*!" he said more loudly now, rising to his feet behind the desk and leaning toward me. "You have no idea who you're fighting, do you? You know *nothing* about the Black Pans!" He paused, breathing deeply. "But soon–soon you will know a great deal about us."

He glanced at the Arab. "Give me her ring."

I began to struggle, but the Arab's iron hands grabbed my wrist, wrenched Pan Fulong's ring off my finger, and handed it to Older Brother.

"You have the same choice as before, back in Shanghai," Older Brother continued abruptly. "Marry into the Black Pans–me, this time, as my third wife. Or death."

I glared at him, trembling.

"Oh, by the way, as you decide, you should know that I do not treat my wives as courteously as my late younger brother. And should you choose death, I will let Hakim here enjoy you in his own peculiar way, first, before killing you very slowly."

Involuntarily my eyes flickered to the Arab, who bared yellow teeth in a smile–or was it a threat?– that turned my stomach.

With a great show Older Brother slipped Pan Fulong's ring onto his little finger. "Ah. It feels right, there," he said contentedly, holding his hand up and admiring the ring. "And I cannot tell you how good it is to have our dear ancestor's spirit tablet back in our ancestor altar, cousin." He inclined his head to the small shrine beside the desk. There, in the recess of the shrine, I could see the tablet glimmer from the light of the incense stick before it. My jaw tightened, and strength and resolve surged into me. My trembling stopped. *This was for the White Pans. For Pan Fulong.*

I glanced at Hawkins, and nodded.

Hawkins stepped forward, and raised his hand, pointing his finger at Older Brother, whose eyes involuntarily focused on the threatening gesture. A contemptuous laugh erupted from his mouth.

Meanwhile, my hand moved to the pendant around my neck, and pressed the ivory ring. I felt the weight of the cloisonne piece settle in my hand as the chain disengaged and the razor blades swiveled open. I twisted my body ever so slowly, and *flung* the throwing star full force at Older Brother.

The star bit deep into his throat before he even saw it coming. His startled gaze locked onto my eyes. A puzzled look came into his eyes for a brief second, before blood erupted from his neck. He pitched forward onto his desk.

As he hit the desk, a black hand emerged from the darkness behind him, grasped the pistol there, and scooped it to Hawkins.

Hawkins caught the pistol from Tabitha in mid-air with both hands, swiveled to his right, and the pistol exploded into the chest of the Arab. A brief, startled look swept the giant's face, also. He staggered back from the impact of the ball, hit the wall behind him, quivered upright for a brief moment, then fell forward full length, hitting the floor with a crash.

Hawkins looked at me, his eyes wide, the pistol still in both hands. "That sound. Just like Billy Bones hitting the parlour floor," he said, awe in his voice.

More Tanka came rushing into the room at the sound of the pistol, knives in hand. This was our moment of truth. I stepped forward, and raised my arm.

"Tanka. Your people have served Black Pans for generations. They are dead now. Will you serve a White Pan?" I stepped forward to the desk, and grabbed Older Brother's limp hand. I slipped the ring off his finger–the second time in a year I had removed my ring from the hand of a dead Black Pan. *I've got to quit doing this*, I thought to myself, as I slipped the ring onto my finger.

Stepping back, I raised my hand and showed them the ring. "This is the seal ring of Pan Fulong, the White Pan, who conferred the honor of serving the Pans upon your distant ancestors, three hundred years ago. Will you serve his descendant once again?"

It wasn't much of a speech. I hadn't thought far enough ahead to rehearse it. I held my breath, waiting for their reply.

I could see them looking at each other in the dim light, the lantern's gleam reflecting off their flat foreheads. A volley of gutteral sounds bubbled up from them, their language as coarse as their appearance. Back and forth the harsh sounds traveled. Behind them, I saw a dark movement, and felt better, having Tabitha back there. Especially with Silver's dirk in her belt.

The oldest Tanka stepped forward in a sudden silence, his broad face impassive. Slowly, deliberately, he brought his two big hands together in front of his face, right hand over left fist, in the old gesture of greeting and obedience. He bowed his head toward me. The others promptly followed suit.

A sigh escaped my lips, and I felt Hawkins' hand on my shoulder. Behind the Tankas, I glimpsed Tabitha's white teeth gleaming in a smile.

"You understand the Shanghai dialect?" I asked the old Tanka.

He nodded, eyes never wavering from my face.

"My first request is this. Tie Older Brother and the Arab together, attach several heavy weights, and dump them overboard, into the harbor."

He bowed. "If your servant may suggest, my Lady," he said in a surprisingly cultured voice. "Should we first search their clothing, and remove any articles of value or identification, should you wish to use them for some purpose in the future?"

I smiled. And made a mental note not to judge the Tankas by their appearances. "Yes. Thank you for the suggestion."

He bowed again. "It shall be done, your ladyship. Should we release your honorable grandfather, and bring him into your auspicious presence?"

"Again, yes," I answered him. He was using the ancient honorific title for me. I decided that I was going to like being a White Pan.

* * * * *

Silver's stateroom was wreathed in smoke. My grandfather had freely contributed his last cigars to the celebration, so Grandfather, Silver, even

Hawkins and Tabitha were puffing away contentedly. Although Hawkins was turning a very interesting shade of yellow as he smoked his first cigar.

"Me hearties, ye've done me proud," Silver was proclaiming as he finished his fourth glass of rum. "Never for a moment did I doubt yore brill'yant plan'd carry the day."

We all laughed at that, remembering his nervous salute as we had left the ship earlier in the evening.

"We cannot thank you enough for your able assistance, all of you," Grandfather said grandly, the copious rum rendering him even more mellow than usual.

"So, your ladyship," Tabitha asked me, with a slight mocking tone. "What are you going to do with your crew of vermin?"

"First thing I'm going to do is never again use the term 'vermin'. They are able and intelligent, despite their appearance. I'd appreciate us all referring to them as 'water folk' or simply 'Tanka'."

Tabitha inclined her head. The others followed suit.

"By thunder, we've two dozen more strong arms to load the Chinee treasure under Del Morro," Silver declared. "And another boat to store it in. That be a help!"

"A help and a danger," said Tabitha quietly. "Our real problem is the eyes in the castle. Meilu's Tanka and their junk will interest those eyes."

That set us all back. She was perfectly right. The last thing we wanted was the exotic junk and my newly acquired crew to attract attention to us as we somehow snuck the treasure out from under the Spaniards' nose.

"Huh. That be a might weighty consid'ration," Silver admitted. He poured himself another rum to help him think it through.

"Difficult to hide that junk," Tabitha observed.

"Silver," I said, before he could add the rum to his total and lose all concentration. "Could you use a dozen able workers at your plantation in the Vinales Valley for a period of time?"

"Use 'em? I'd welcome 'em," he grandly proclaimed, then gulped the rum before I could interrupt him again.

"Thank you. I'm inclined to slip the junk out of the harbor at first light, as soon as the chain is dropped. I don't much relish explaining everything to the Commandante. Be gone before he realizes it, sail to Punta Gorda, then dock the junk there for the time being. Lodge the crew at Silver's plantation."

"And return here," finished Tabitha, "to help us solve our problem. How to smuggle several hundred chests of Chinese treasure onto the *Pieces of Eight*. Out from under Del Morro castle. Past the Spaniards."

"By thunder, I'll drink to that!" Silver bellowed, and poured himself, then all of us, more rum.

Hawkins stood abruptly and dropped his cigar, his color having progressed from yellow to green, and wobbled toward the door. "I think I'll get some fresh air on deck," he squeaked, amid much laughter all around.

Chapter Fourteen. Jim Interrupts Swordplay

The next two days were the most miserable of my short English life. Not even in the cold, rain-pelted early spring days at the Admiral Benbow had I felt so poorly. How a cigar that smelled so fine could make me feel so poorly was a great mystery, which I had ample opportunity to ponder.

Meilu had returned from Punta Gorda at the end of the two days. Finally, the morning after, we all rose with the sun, and applied ourselves to the treasure problem. Long John had anchored us in the middle of the harbor, so that we had a clear view of the entire bay as we gathered on deck to consider how to snatch the Chinese treasure from the sea cave.

"Here be the problem, mateys," Long John said to myself, Meilu, and Tabitha on the waist of the deck. "A great treasure rests 'neath that most formidable castle"–here he pointed to the imposing stone mass of Del Morro, astraddle the high cliff of the east side of the bay's mouth. "A castle that be swarmin' with Spaniards, their eyes roaming over every inch of the bay. We needs to transfer that treasure into our hands–most likely onto this here *Pieces of Eight*."

"I suppose the most direct way," offered Meilu, "would be to just anchor the *Pieces of Eight* outside the bay beside the cave, and ferry the chests by longboat straight to it–our route that first night that we discovered the sea cave."

"Aye, that'd be the most direct," admitted Long John. "But I'm thinking the *Pieces of Eight* be mighty visible, sittin' just offshore of the castle day after day. Longboats running to and fro with nary a pause–"

"Sailors lugging strange-looking chests from the longboats up to the deck," I added.

"Not to mention that the sea outside th' bay be often rough, and those waters too deep to throw an anchor into," concluded Long John, with a long face.

"Eyes from the castle would quickly spy the activity, and be curious," Tabitha stated flatly. "The treasure would not be ours for long."

"Aye, you may lay to that," admitted Long John glumly.

"So we do it at night," I remarked. "The darkness covers us."

Meilu shook her head. "Only at night? Only when we have low tides? Only when the sea is calm? It will take us forever."

Silence.

"What alternatives do we have?" I asked.

"Why not hide ourselves by being conspicuous?" Tabitha asked. "There are hundreds of ships in the harbor. Anchor the *Pieces of Eight* in the middle of the harbor–right where we are now–and move the treasure in the day."

Long John laughed. "Aye, I likes your way of thinking, my dearie. The bay's waters are calm, and will take an anchor. My ship would not stand out. But it's a far piece from the sea cave to here–we'd wear ourselves out with the rowin'."

"And still be conspicuous lifting the chests from the longboat to the deck," I added.

"Well, that will always be a problem," observed Meilu.

"Unless–nobody notices cargo being loaded onto a ship from a *dock*," I thought out loud. "Why not load the lacquer chests from a dock?"

"Int'restin'," Long John mused. "That'd solve one problem. But we've still got to get the blamed chests to the dock without attractin' attention."

"So what's the closest dock to the sea cave?" I asked.

"There ain't any," Long John answered with a sour face. He pointed to the heart of the city. "City wharves, from Plaza de Armas to Plaza Vieja–clear across the whole bloody bay from the sea cave." He pointed further south. "Atares Inlet docks–even farther away, and restricted by the Governor-General for galleon construction."

"Those are docks over there–the end of the bay?" Meilu asked.

"Aye, the Guanacaboa docks. Monstrous far away, and miserable docks with miserable roads leadin' to 'em."

A pall descended over us.

"No docks at all close to the mouth of the bay?" I persisted, turning around to stare at the bay's entrance.

"Nay," answered Long John.

"What's that?" Tabitha asked, her keen eyes and long finger directed at the base of Del Morro Castle.

Long John threw back his head, laughing long and loud. It took him a moment to recover. "Aye, my dearie, yore sharp eyes found a dock, all right." More laughter shook him, and he nearly fell off his crutch. "But those be the docks of Del Morro Castle itself, dearie! The Commandante's private, exclusive dock, to provision his castle."

I looked more closely where Tabitha's finger pointed.

"Is that a road snaking down the cliff from the castle to the dock?" I asked.

"To be sure," Long John answered. "A might fine road, I hear. Zig-zags from the dock up to the very gate of the Castle, around the shoulder of the rampart, there."

"And at the castle gate, the road continues on, around the bay to the city?" I wondered.

"Aye, that it does," Long John answered. "A good road, too. I traveled it, only once. To claim Isaiah from the dungeon o' the Castle. I had won 'im with a special pair of dice I was might partial to, by thunder. Tho' I wondered whether I'd gained anything of value, when I picked the boy up from the Castle. He was a sight that shivered me timbers, he was. More dead 'n alive."

No one had much to say about that.

Long John cast a sharp look at me, then Tabitha, as we stared at the far-away dock.

"Put it out of yore minds, mateys. That dock's right under the Commandante's nose. It's the last place we want to be loadin' our treasure. Not to mention the last dock we'd have any reason to visit in the run o' things. We'd stand out monstrous, having no call to be anywhere close to there."

"Silver's right," Meilu concluded. "That's the last dock we would want to load our treasure from. Or have a plausible excuse to be visiting."

"Which brings us back to Hawkins' first idea," Tabitha remarked. "My time–night. Darkness covering the *Pieces of Eight.* Outside the harbor. Right next to the sea cave."

"Restricted to nighttime low tides, with no anchor possible, so only in calm seas," Meilu summarized glumly. "Shouldn't take us more than a decade. Maybe two."

Long John shifted on his crutch, his eyes going from one to the other of us. No one liked the prospect, but it seemed we were stuck with it. At least until a better plan came along–which seemed highly unlikely.

Long John slapped his hand on the railing. "We needs some cheering up, mateys," he observed with a forced show of enthusiasm. "Let's lunch at a charming little restaurant off the Plaza de Armas. The Cafe Dominica specializes in exotic preserves served over sweet biscuits–not hearty, but a wondrous variety of tastes! And their *gara pina* drink–fermented pineapple extract that'd make a man forget all his cares!"

* * * * *

The Cafe Dominica lived up to the expectations Long John had aroused in us. Indeed, it was grand enough to be found in London, I thought, which brought to mind my mother and Dr. Livesey, and prompted a secret smile on my face.

The owner greeted Long John as a long-lost friend, and guided us to a table next to the fountain of jasper stone in the center of the courtyard. Marble floor tiles and waiters in black furthered the elegant feel of the place.

Once the platter of hot biscuits arrived with the dozen bowls of different preserves to slather over them, we set to with determination. As always, Long John was the merriest of the lot, though in truth all of us were having a grand time. Shortly after the *gara pina* drinks arrived, we had put our unease over transferring the Chinese treasure quite behind us, as the biscuits disappeared at a rapid clip.

I was in a seat facing the entrance, and so saw it first. The Commandante appeared, with a jeweled lady in green and gold on his arm. I touched Meilu's hand, inclined my head toward the entrance, and watched her eyes grow wide as the handsome pair was escorted toward the far side of the courtyard by the owner. Halfway there, the Commandante glanced our direction, and abruptly stopped in shock. His face reddened, and he changed course to approach our table.

"Long John," I said in an urgent whisper. "Storm to starboard."

Long John's second, or perhaps third, glass of *gara pina* paused before his mouth. His laugh died abruptly as the Commandante arrived at our table.

"Why, Commandante. What a surprise," said Long John, uneasily.

"Surprise, Captain Silver? Surely it is my place to be surprised, to see a slave sitting at table in a respectable cafe?"

"Mind your tongue, sir," Long John replied, heat in his voice. "The lady is a free woman, purchased by meself, and a respected member of our party."

Now Long John was as good a liar as I ever saw, but mainly the Commandante's surprise and rising anger were to account for his not recognizing Tabitha in her colorful garb. The Commandante's eyes swept the table. "Indeed? And a most peculiar party it is, with every mongrel race on the planet represented. All that is missing is the civilized presence of a Spaniard."

Long John pulled himself up from his chair with his crutch, and shoved it under his left arm. The alcohol in the *gara pinas* made him unsteady, and his temper had risen quickly.

"A Spaniard would but lower the level of this here table, Commandante, you may lay to that!" he bellowed, surging toward the Commandante.

Meilu and I had risen, and quickly grabbed Long John by the arms, holding him back.

The Commandante's pretty companion, jealous at his attention shifting away from her, pulled on the Commandante's arm to go. The

Commandante reluctantly turned his venomous gaze from Long John's swaying figure, and made to depart with her.

In a voice not lowered but in fact louder than normal, the Commandante leaned toward his companion's dainty ear, where a string of diamonds dangled. "Captain Silver is quite enamored of the negroes. They say he sleeps with one–a cripple yet!"

"Belay that talk!!" Long John roared, shaking off Meilu and me as he hobbled furiously around the table, showering curses on the Commandante. The ring of steel filled the courtyard as first Long John and quickly the Commandante drew their swords.

Long John was the first to attack, a sweeping series of cuts which the Commandante easily parried, even with his short sword and the beauty still on his arm. The ringing clash of their blades sent diners scurrying away in all directions, as chairs toppled this way and that.

The Commandante gently pushed his companion away, and with a cold smile began to circle around Long John, who was red in the face and trembling with anger.

"Quickly," Meilu whispered in my ear. "He deliberately provoked Silver, and will kill him easily."

Meilu and I rushed forward, grabbed Long John by his shoulders, and dragged him back. Meilu pulled his sword arm down, pinning it to his body. Long John struggled against us, but we had him safely back and away from the Commandante.

The Commandante raised an eyebrow, but rather than withdrawing, he suddenly raised his sword and, stepping toward us, made to plunge it into Long John's chest.

My pistol was out from my belt in a second, and my outstretched arm leveled it at the Commandante's eyes as I pulled the hammer back.

"Another step and you're dead," I said, in a voice whose firmness surprised me. "I've killed before, sir, and I'm perfectly capable of doing so again."

The Commandante came to an abrupt halt, his bulging eyes set on the pistol not a yard from his face. The water gurgling from the fountain behind us was the only sound in the courtyard. Somehow, amazingly, my hand and the pistol were completely steady before the Commandante's face, my finger tight on the trigger.

He stood, stunned, for some seconds. Slowly he backed away, even as I held the pistol still aimed at his face. Slowly, deliberately, he lowered his sword and put it back in its sheath. His eyes never wavered from my pistol, as he spoke to Long John.

"You have been saved, for now, Captain Silver. You are very fortunate I am in the company of a beautiful woman, rather than my soldiers. This is a private affair between you and me, but it has not ended–of that you may be sure."

He turned, offered his arm to the woman, who unsteadily took it, and stiffly walked across the silent courtyard to his table, where he clapped his hands for service.

Long John stood, breathing heavily, as waiters hurried to the Commandante's table, and other diners cautiously returned to their tables. I lowered my pistol, and carefully released the hammer. My hand was trembling badly, now. Long John returned his sword to its scabbard, and hobbled back to his seat. We all sat, but eating was far from our minds.

"Tabitha, me dearie, by the powers, I don't know how much longer you and I can stand that Spanish pig," Long John muttered.

"We have a treasure to reclaim first," Meilu observed. "But after that trifling question is resolved, by all means let us ponder the Commandante's fate."

Long John took a deep breath. "Jim, my lad, it seems I owes you a favor," said he. "Now that I considers it, cool like, you and that pistol probably saved my life, by thunder. Thankee kindly, my boy."

"My pleasure, Long John," I replied. "I remember well when you gave me this pistol, at your inn in Bristol, about a year ago."

"Let's be off," he said. "Suddenly I don't much like the air in here," with a glance at the Commandante's table on the other side of the courtyard. He tossed two gold doubloons onto the table.

As we rose to leave, Long John grabbed a handful of the remaining biscuits. His eyes met mine.

"Worked up a new appytite, I did, matey," he said with a weak smile. "No sense letting these beauties go to waste now, is there?"

Chapter Fifteen. Long John's Tale

'He's no common man, Long John,' said the coxswain Israel Hands to me. 'He had good schooling in his young days, and can speak like a book when so minded; and brave–a lion's nothing alongside of Long John!' – Ch. 10, Treasure Island, *by Robert Louis Stevenson*

I was in Long John's cabin aboard the *Pieces of Eight*, watching him wolf down the last of the biscuits from the Cafe Dominica. He cast one of his shrewd glances my direction.

"I don't reckon my eating these biscuits is what you're int'rested in, me boy."

I was fidgeting with the sextant on his desk, and made my fingers stop being nervous. "You said back at the cafe that you owed me a favor. I'd like to cash it in, Long John."

He laughed, licking the last of the biscuits off his fingers. "Fire away, young Jim Hawkins. What suits your fancy? Me ship? Me first mate? You can have anything you want, boy, 'cepting my wife." He threw back his head and laughed.

I let the laugh die out, then steeled myself.

"I've got everything I need already, Long John. What I want is to know how you came to be a pirate. And how you came to have Lady Silver as your wife."

He stared at me, shocked-like. In truth, I don't rightly remember ever seeing him more surprised.

Instantly sober, the old buccaneer began playing with the sextant himself for a long moment. Then he shoved it away.

"Ye're a hard man, Jim Hawkins. By the powers, outside of my missus, I don't reckon there's more'n a couple of men alive–other than me'self–that knows that horrible tale."

I began to think he was going to refuse me, and mustered some arguments in my head to force him.

"But if that's the favor ye want, by thunder, that's what I be required to give ye," he said, pulling himself up by his crutch and beginning to hobble around the stateroom. He stopped, stared out the stern window, and began to talk, his back to me.

"I was most like a spitting image of you as a lad, boy. Smart as paint, I was told. Handsome, even, if you can believe that. But so they said. My dad, he run an inn in Bristol, and run it darn good, by the powers. He learned me everything he knew, which was a sight, and sent me off for schooling for even more.

"By the time he worked hisself and my mother to death at the inn, I was a rising star in the East India Company. The Company sent me off to set up a trading station in the Bight of Benin, in the Gulf of Guinea in Africa. They was noticing the Spaniards' staggering profits in the slave trade there, and figured they could complement their spice profits from India with black gold from Africa.

"Anyways, I went. Overseed the building of a fort on Lagos Island, smack in the middle of Yoruba country. The king there, Akinsemoyin, was called the *Oba of Lagos,* and styled himself a right god-king. Couldn't no one talk to him or even lay eyes on him. So I worked with his *Otun*, a kind of right-hand man, hisself a lower chief. Name of Ketere. Otun Ketere, we called him. Happy enough, they was, to have us there, 'cause we increased their profits considerably from their slave trade with enemy tribes, above what the Spaniards was doing already. The head of the Spanish there was a likable young fellow named Cacigal, who quickly became a drinking mate of mine–it were powerful lonely on Lagos Island, my boy.

"Well, it warn't long before me and Cacigal noticed that Otun Ketere had a daughter, maybe five years younger'n us. That girl was the most beautiful thing we'd ever seen, tall and slim, danced like no one I ever seen, before or since, and a mind like quicksilver, with a smile that made ya feel that everything was dead-on right with the world."

Long John hobbled around on his crutch, to facing me. "Ye can't know what I mean when I says that, I 'spect, young Jim. Someday you will. But it's a might powerful feeling, that smile from a lass that makes ya feel that everything is dead-on right with the world. Well, Cacigal's mom and dad were still alive, and he knew what they'd think about a black daughter-in-law, even if she was a princess, the daughter of a chief. Mine were dead, as I've said, so I assumed they'd be all right with it, and proposed our marriage to her father, Otun Ketere. He said no, of course. Wanted to keep the girl close to him, and I don't blame him for that. It set me and my girl back a bit, it did. But we figured we'd just have to convince him, somehow.

"By this time, I'd grown disgusted with the slave trade. Ye can't imagine, my lad, how evil the trade is, how it brings down ever'thing it touches. Including, I may say, Otun Ketere, though he was the father of the girl I loved. Well, I determined to find other products from the Gulf of Guinea for the Company to make their profits from. I traveled east along the Gulf into the Niger Delta, and spent some time in Calabar, where I discovered mahogany and teak plantations–the wood not quite as profitable as slaves, but a sight less perishable and–well, easier on the mind.

"I was feeling mighty good as I rushed back to Lagos Island to arrange for our ships to begin calling at Calabar for hardwoods instead of for slaves at Lagos. When I got there, I discovered..."

Here Long John choked up, and stood gritting his teeth for some moments.

"Well. Cacigal told me how the *Oba* king had gotten convinced by someone that Chief Ketere was shaving some of his profits from him. Maybe it was so, maybe not. But The *Oba* had gotten a new *Otun* while I was gone, and sold Ketere and his family onto the next slave ship out–a Spanish one, as it happens. The ship was gone by the time Cacigal realized what had happened, long gone by the time I returned from Calabar.

"That were a bad day in me life, Jim Hawkins, and you may lay to that.

The next week weren't no better. No one kept tidy records on the cargo of slavers. I never did find where my girl was sent to–somewheres on the Spanish Main, but it's a right big area, from Cartagena to Maracaibo to Veracruz to Hispaniola to Havana. A right big area. But I did know that near half the cargo of slavers died before reaching the Caribbean, and a sight more of those the women than the men.

"So I figured I'd lost the thing that meant most to me in my life. And being young, and hot-blooded, I couldn't let it lay like that. Before I knowed what I'd done, I'd decided that there weren't nothing left in life for me but revenge. And revenge meant killing as many Spaniards on the Spanish Main as I could lay me hands on. I ships out to the Caribbean, and within the month signed on with Capt'n English, whose pirate crew was killing monstrous numbers of Spaniards up and down the Spanish Main. We hit Maracaibo, Trujillo, Campeche, Santo Domingo, and dozens of ships sailing to and from those poor towns. It were a lot of cuttin' and rippin', lad, ten years or so, and I'm ashamed to say it felt powerful good. Powerful good."

He hobbled over to his desk, and slumped into the chair there, looking old and tired to my eyes, just from the telling of it. I began to feel bad about asking him about it, and a bit sick in the pit of my stomach, from what I'd heard.

He took a long drink of rum from the bottle on the table, and began again, in a weak, tired voice.

"The Articles with Capt'n English ran their course, and we disbanded. I was rich from my share–had risen to be his quarter-master, I had. I quick signed on with Flint after that. The killing and drink and all had got in my blood, I'm ashamed to say. With my girl gone, there weren't nothing else in life for me. Flint was even worse than English. It was while we was ransacking Cartagena that I found her. I had just slit the throat of a big innkeeper, and glanced around the room, when I saw her, cowering behind the bar. It didn't take more'n a second for us to recognize each other. Oh, we'd changed, we had. I was covered in blood, and mighty fierce-looking, I suppose. And my girl, when I rushed around the bar to get her in my arms–she was crippled, her hips and legs crushed by the ballast on the slave ship shifting in a storm, she told me. It didn't matter to me, not a whit. She was still my girl, and though I didn't deserve it, I was still her man.

"I put her in my quarter-master cabin until we hit the next port, said I'd kill any man that touched her, then sent her to Bristol with all my loot from Capt'n English. She convinced me to give up the pirating–said to me, straight out, it was making me as bad as the slavers. I knowed she was right, and wanted to quit then and there. But Flint wouldn't let me out. Pointed out, in that convincin' way of his, that I'd signed the Articles for five years, and that I still had two years to go. It might've cost me my life, to try and quit early. So I stayed for two more years, while my girl bought the inn at Bristol and run it.

"Not long after she'd left for Bristol, we took on a ship that had a platoon of marines on it. That were a fight, let me tell you. That were where Pew lost his eyes, and me my leg. A ball from a four inch cannon ripped it off. One moment it was there, and the next it warn't. It were a punishment, for all my black deeds. I knowed that, and I was all right with it. So was my girl, when we exchanged letters about it. We were both crippled by the things that had happened to us. It were hard, but that be the way of the world, Jim. It's a rough world, and you have to be might lucky to get through it whole, and you may lay to that.

"Anyways, the two years was finally up. Flint sails to Savannah, finishes drinking hisself to death, and we takes our shares and splits up. I'm straight to Bristol, reunited with my girl, and things is all right with the world. Then Black Dog and Pew shows up, says they've found Billy Bones, who's got Flint's Fist–the treasure map from his early days–and do I want to jine 'em. No ways, says I. Like I say, I got my girl, and I'm happy. They track Billy Bones to your inn down on the West Devon coast, Jim, and I reckon you knows the story from there. They miss the map by minutes, finding Billy sprawled on your parlour floor dead as steel. They think it's all over, and so do I, and glad of it. Then your Squire shows up not a fortnight later, blabbin' all over Bristol how he's got Flint's map and looking for a crew to help find the treasure.

"It were too much for me to resist, lad. I reckon losing my leg weren't quite enough punishment for me. My girl urged me against it, but I had too much pirate in me to pass up Flint's treasure, when I had but to lift my hand to take it, or so I thought. Against her wishes, I signs on the *Hispaniola*, and sails to Treasure Island with you and the Squire and the good Doctor Livesey. And as we sail, and away from my girl, I get near as bad as I ever was. Though you mind, do you not, Jim Hawkins, how I saved your life from George Merry and Israel Hands and the others on more'n one occasion? Do you mind that, Jim?"

I nodded. It was true. But I was feeling horrible, as I relived those days on Treasure Island. And remembered seeing Long John stick a knife in poor Tom's back on that beach, and hearing him plot to kill a sight more, as I hid in the apple barrel on the *Hispaniola's* deck.

Long John could see what I was feeling. He rushed on. "But all that be water behind the stern, m' boy. Past and done for, or near as anything in life is done for. Afterwards, I escapes the attentions of your Squire, make it here to Cuba, and send for my missus. She sells the inn at Bristol, and we're soon together in Havana, with all my wealth from English and Flint, more'n enough to buy a pretty tobaccy plantation in the Vinales Valley, and this here *Pieces of Eight* to boot."

"But Long John," I said, rousing myself out of the black mood that was threatening me. "Why did the Spaniards here take you in? They know who you are. They must know how you and English and Flint plundered their ships and towns all over the Spanish Main."

He leaned back his head and laughed. "Aye, boy, you would think they'd have me on the gallows quicker'n the Squire would!" He slapped the table and laughed some more. "But two things changed their minds, lad. They knowed the Squire and the British wanted to hang me, and they figures that any enemy of the British is a friend of their'n." He laughed again, and poured himself another rum, which he promptly downed.

"And for the second, it just happens that the current Governor-General ruling over Cuba is me old drinking mate from Lagos Island, none other than Cacigal!" Another roar of laughter from Long John, and now a bout of slapping his thighs, so that he's about helpless with merriment at the thought, though not so helpless but what he can't pour himself another glass of rum and drink it in one swallow, between laughs.

•

I wait until he calms down a bit, thinking.

"So that's why you free your slaves, and treat them so decent," I observed.

"Aye, that's so. I've got my girl and I've got my *Pieces of Eight*, by thunder, so I don't rightly want or need more in life. But my girl, she worries about the next life a bit, she does. Not so much as to ruin this one, but she thinks about it. She figures every slave I free balances out the sheet a bit from all the people I've killed."

"Do you think so, Long John?"

He shook his head, looking old again. "Her and her *orishas.* Do I believe in another world, full of *orishas,* that give a whit about what we do down here? I don't know, lad. Maybe. But those *orishas* seem to have all the vices and passions that we do down here. Where's the progress there?"

I nodded. "And what about Meilu, and her dead folk with monstrous dollops of *ch'i* energy you can call on?"

He laughed and poured himself another rum. He studied the gold liquor in the glass. "That's not so all-fire of a stretch, for me. Flint, I know he's dead, saw his stiff grey body in Savannah. But that man did have a way about him. An air about him. Call it *ch'i,* whatever. And I can imagine some of that energy sticking around for a whiles, I can."

"You know what, Long John? That *Ma Tsu* gal is intriguing."

He slugged the drink down. "Yeah. Know what ya mean, lad. Funny, we English think of the sea as threat'nin', a great challenge to overcome, most of us'n. A battle to be fought, no end of it. But ya know, boy. I thinks of the sea a bit diff'rent. Like a strong but temper'mental friend. Got to be wary around him. But–I likes him. Feel good in his company. I likes being on a ship, with the wind pushing me forwards. Which seems to be a bit o' the way Meilu thinks of *Ma Tsu* and the sea. Dangerous, maybe. But not threat'nin'."

I nod. *The wind fills my heart as well as the sails. The salt in my blood calls to the salt of the sea, whose answer wraps me in an ancient embrace. I am at home, where I belong, at peace in the mystery of it all.*

It seemed to me that maybe what really mattered was what you did in your life, whether you called on *orishas* or dark-faced ladies or nothing at all.

"So–you think maybe Lady Silver is right, finally, Long John? That every slave you free balances out every man you've killed?"

He shrugged, cast a long look at the bottle, and put the cork back in it, to my considerable surprise.

"Who the devil knows? I only knows two things, Jim Hawkins. I know I love my girl, and she's with me. I know I love sailing the seas, and I've got a ship to do it in. A copper-bottomed ship, yet, thanks to you and Flint's silver bars. I don't give a rip about anything else, lad. Not a rip. I figure I'll live out my days, and when I dies the devil and the *orishas* can do whatever they wants with me–if there is a devil, and if there's anything left of me. Until then, I'm a happy man, and that's a sight more'n many can say, by thunder."

So that was Silver's tale. In truth, I hardly knew how much to believe of it. I did know this, though. That Lady Silver had the bearing of a princess, and that Long John Silver treated his freed slaves as right as any could wish. Gradually, with misgivings, I began to understand the old buccaneer and his murdering days. I even, God forgive me, began to like the fellow, against all my judgment.

Orishas and dark-faced ladies, I hadn't figured out. Probably never will.

Chapter Sixteen. Tabitha's Discovery

I settle into the high window alcove. I'm rubbing momma's *Obatala* amulet for luck. My pocket bulges with a *mamey colorado* from the Mandinka woman in the Plaza Vieja. In the room below, the Count of Jaruco is doing paperwork at his huge desk. The desk is very neat and clean. Unusual for a Spaniard.

Dare I eat the fruit in my pocket? Decide no. Two weeks ago, in the plaza outside, I became careless, and was very nearly caught by the Commandante. Only because *Obatala* sent me my strange new companions am I here, waiting for the Commandante's weekly meeting with the Count. Instead of in the dungeons of Del Morro Castle.

He enters. From my high shadows, he seems nervous, excited. I lean to the edge of the shadow, eyes and ears alert. The stone is cool beneath my hand.

"Commandante, my good friend!" says the Count, pushing aside his papers. "You are beaming! A new mistress, you handsome devil?"

A laugh from the Commandante. "Even better, my friend. Finally that English dog will be safely in my Del Morro dungeons, where my men can torture him for their amusement."

My pulse quickens. I hold my breath, waiting for an explanation.

"Aha! What did he do, to come into your fond embrace?"

Another laugh. "He does not know it yet, but tomorrow I will publicly apprehend the one-legged pirate attempting to smuggle rum onto his ship, and send him to the dungeons for violating the declaration of duties on that good product."

"Indeed. Most ingenious. But Silver only deals in tobacco, does he not?"

"So he thinks," the Commandante whispers.

I lean forward, to catch the low conversation.

"But tomorrow, when his first wagonload of tobacco stops for inspection at the city gates, his wagoneer will become carelessly distracted by some pretty girls, and my men will insert a case of rum into the wagon. When the wagon reaches the docks for loading onto his ship, I myself will appear to accept his declaration of duties. He will declare the tobacco, but not, of course, the hidden rum. I search the wagon to verify the declaration of duties, discover the rum, and clap the pirate in irons on the spot!"

The two men laugh loudly. The Count pours two glasses–not of rum, I notice, but his expensive Spanish port.

"A masterful plot, my devious friend!" the Count shouts. "A toast, to your cleverness, and the eminent dispatch of Long John Silver to the dungeons of Del Morro Castle!"

I fall back into the alcove, in shock. Glasses clink below.

"Yes, to the deepest dungeons I have," the Commandante gloats. "Filthy water, rats, lice on the threadbare mattress, and a very disturbed sergeant whose only pleasure in life is inflicting pain on others."

More laughter, more clinking of glasses.

The Commandante groans in pleasure. "Yes, only one thing could increase my happiness."

"And what is that, my friend?"

"Putting his friends in the dungeons with him. Particularly his slaves. I do believe if I could find an excuse to put his first mate there with him, and that new young girl who dresses so colorfully, I'd shove my sergeant aside and take over the torturing myself."

"My friend, your plan is masterful. Simple, direct, fool-proof. Even Silver's old friend the Governor-General won't be able to intervene for someone caught red-handed smuggling rum to sell abroad. After all, the duties on exported products are the only real source of funds supporting the Governor-General and all his staff."

"Yes, yes. I had to do something, after Silver's unprovoked attack on me at the Cafe Dominica yesterday–you heard of that, I presume?"

"Of course. There is no other topic of conversation in Havana society. We marvel at how easily you out-dueled him, how cravenly he was saved by the upstart English boy."

"Yes, yes, quite unsporting," observes the Commandante. "Downright un-Spanish. But what can you expect from blacks and Englishmen? The episode inspired me to be rid of the lot of them, and quickly."

The Count pours more port. "Well, thanks to your brilliance, by this time tomorrow, the old pirate will be in the hands of your sadistic sergeant in the dungeon, and it will only be a matter of time before you find some pretext to have him joined there by his slaves."

The Commandante accepts the port, and throws it down in one swallow. "Yes, his slaves, and the English boy. And that Chinese girl. Soon. I'll find a way."

I've heard enough. While the two men talk on below me, I slip through the window bars, past the house martin nest, where four chicks are clamoring for food, and slide down the gutter. Soon I am through the vendors of the Plaza Vieja and moving up Mercaderes toward the harbor. My heart is beating fast, and my mind racing the same speed. My friends are a day from the Commandante's dungeon.

And I am two days away from the same.

Chapter Seventeen. Jim Learns to Plot

"Aarghhh!!" Long John's scream filled the stateroom. We all shrank back as he lunged for his sword, whipped it out of the scabbard, and proceeded to slash viciously as he lurched about the room on his crutch, mighty oaths accompanying every stroke of the blade. I had heard Long John's curses on the *Hispaniola* and on the *Pieces of Eight*, as well as Treasure Island, and today he surpassed himself.

Tabitha had just related to our astonished ears the plot she had overheard from the Commandante. Long John's rage spent itself in half a minute, during which he had bellowed an impressive catalogue of the Commandante's vile traits and low ancestry. I am a born Englishman, and not dull, yet his colorful vocabulary stretched even my knowledge. He paused before the stern window, searching for more curses, and had taken a deep breath to start in anew, when Meilu's calm voice interrupted him.

"It's perfectly simple, after all," she said quietly. "After his men secretly load the rum at the city gate, we stop within the city, at my home, for example, unload it, and watch the Commandante's astonishment when he fails to find his rum in the wagon at the docks. My father will much appreciate a case of the Commandante's rum."

Long John whirled around, let the comment sink in, then a short laugh burst from his mouth, followed by a quite longer laugh, followed by a roar of delight. He slashed the air with his sword a couple of more times, but now in playfulness.

"No!"

Tabitha's outburst brought us up short.

"Not simply unload his rum from the wagon," she said, white teeth flashing in a grin from her dark face. "Substitute his case of rum with a case of water. From the spring you're always talking about in your home!"

"Yes! Yes!" continued Meilu. "So that the arrogant schemer knows we discovered his plot, and have plotted him one better yet! He'll be so confused, so embarrassed, so–"

"Angry," I finished for her, a sudden idea sending my skin tingling. "And we'll use that anger, provoke him to banish Long John's ship from loading his tobacco on the city docks."

A stunned silence. I let it hang over the room. The sword dropped from Long John's hand, and clattered onto the floor..

"My boy, have ye taken leave of your senses? What's the point in preventin' me tobaccy from gettin' loaded onto me ship?"

"He's required as harbor-master to make a berth available on some dock to load products that are paying duties, right?"

"Aye, but so what?"

"So he'll be angry–furious, in fact–when we make a fool of him over the smuggled rum. There'll be a scene. You dare him to punish you by banishing you from the favored city docks–banishing you instead to the worst docks in the harbor for loading your tobacco–the Del Morro Castle docks clear across the Bay, a full day away on muddy roads."

Another stunned silence. Again, I let it hang, rather enjoying their puzzlement. Predictably, it was Meilu who figured it out.

"He banishes the *Pieces of Eight* to the Del Morro Castle dock," she repeats, eyes shining, cheeks flushed. "Which gives us a perfect reason to be moored at that dock and loading barrels onto our ship. But some of those barrels–"

"Are not filled with tobacco," broke in Tabitha, white teeth flashing in another grin. "But are filled with the Chinese treasure, which we've ferried from the nearby sea cave just around the mouth of the Bay."

"Keeping our longboats close to the cliff face, where they're invisible to the eyes at the Castle and its ramparts," I added. "We arrive at the Del Morro Castle dock after but a short trip from the sea cave, hoist the tobacco barrels, filled with lacquer chests of treasure, from the longboat onto the dock–"

"And let them mingle with me truc barrels of tobaccy, loading them onto me ship whenever we darn well likes!" burst out Long John.

"Rum!" he roared, hobbling to the door of the stateroom and bellowing up the passageway outside. "More rum, Isaiah! Me brilliant friends here have got the Chinee treasure out of the sea cave and onto me ship, and we're all going to be rich, by the powers!"

We young ones allowed ourselves but one rum, and that diluted with an equal dose of the excellent clean water from Meilu's spring, which she kept in brown bottles on the ship these days. We had planning to do.

"Will the lacquer Chinese chests fit into the tobacco barrels?" Meilu enquired.

"Aye, easily," claimed Long John, who was drinking his rum straight. "We uses the big hogshead barrels for the tobaccy. I'll bet we can stack three or four of the Chinese chests into each hogshead, and you may lay to that."

"Hawkins has had a brilliant idea," Meilu cautioned. "But let's be clear–it's possible the Commandante might occasionally show up at the Castle dock–right, Captain Silver?"

Long John set his glass on the table, and reached for the bottle of rum. Tabitha shoved it away before he could touch it.

"Aye," he said, with an irritated look at the out-of-reach bottle. "Aye, he might be there on and off, I would guess, say every day or two. I imagine his fat lieutenant might be there most every day, supervising the unloading of provisions for the castle from their own boats. That's what the dock be normally used for, after all."

"That makes me nervous," admitted Meilu.

"Be nervous. But be steady," said Tabitha. "My experience is this. If you're steady, you can be right in front of their eyes, and they won't notice. One fact is key. We will have a reason to be at that dock, loading barrels onto our ship. They cannot imagine only some of the barrels contain tobacco. They cannot dream of Chinese treasure from three hundred years ago in some barrels."

Meilu nodded. "Yes. I understand. It still makes me nervous."

Tabitha grinned back at her. "That's what makes it fun."

"Long John," said I, fixing him with a serious look. "This all depends on you using the Commandante's anger to get what we want. It will be tricky. A hundred things could go wrong. You'll have to be wily, dare him to banish us to that dock as if you don't expect him to do it. Try to make him think it's his idea, not yours. Try to make him think that's the last thing you want him to do to you."

Long John nodded slowly. "Aye. His idea. Something that'll hurt me. Drive me to ruin." A grin spread over his face. "I reckon I'm going to enjoy this little theater tomorrow, by thunder."

Tabitha and I grinned. Meilu didn't, a worried look on her face. A hundred things could go wrong, after all. And it looked like she was already imagining most of them.

* * * * *

I sat with Isaiah in the front of the wagon as we approached the Havana city gate, the new sun rising before us. We had intercepted the wagon from Vinales Valley yesterday evening, and taken the reins for the rest of the journey. A dozen of the big tobacco hogshead barrels lay in the wagon under a tarp. The smell was still heavenly, but my first cigar had cured me of smoking. At least for now. Isaiah glanced my direction as he wearily pulled back on the reins and the mules stopped at the gate.

The Commandante's lieutenant himself emerged from the gatehouse, looking as nervous as Isaiah was tired. He waddled up to us.

"Name and destination and load!" he barked, looking back. Two girls emerged from the gatehouse, very heavily made up, and sauntered toward us.

"Uh, Isaiah, and Jim, headed for Captain Silver's ship on the city docks. A dozen hogsheads of, uh, tobacco," Isaiah stammered, pretending to be distracted by the women. As they got close to us, it was pretty clear that he wasn't pretending. The girls in fact were very pretty, and smiling quite warmly at him. Isaiah wasn't acting, but they meant nothing to me, and I had to force myself to appear smitten. We were both under strict orders from Meilu and Tabitha–ignore whatever was going on in the back of the wagon, no matter how clumsy the Commandante's men were.

"We'll have to inspect your load," the fat lieutenant said much too loudly. "Look under the tarp there, men," he said stiffly, as if reading an unfamiliar speech. Then he awkwardly stepped back, to allow the two girls plenty of room to show off their charms.

As the girls simpered and cooed and smiled, the Commandante's men made a racket behind us. To make it seem reasonable we didn't hear all the noise of something obviously being loaded atop the barrels back there, Isaiah began to banter with the girls, asking where they lived, if they had boyfriends, and some other very stupid questions. For the fat lieutenant and the girls, though, no question was too stupid or obviously calculated. I pretended to be as fascinated with the girls as Isaiah, trying hard not to glance back at the source of the commotion behind us.

Meanwhile, Lieutenant Sanchez' eyes were doing enough nervous glancing toward the back of the wagon for all three of us. With undisguised relief he saw the tarp pulled back down and tied off.

"So! Enough!" he snapped at the girls. "Be off–can't you see we have official business here?" He smiled broadly and, I thought, smugly at Isaiah and me. "You're right. Nothing but tobacco barrels in the wagon," he said loudly, still following his script. "You were right, hah hah!" He stepped back, and grandly waved us through the stone gate into the city. "Feel free to go to the dock, with your tobacco barrels!"

Once through the gate, Isaiah and I rolled our eyes at the comical performance, and urged the mules to a quicker walk, which of course was quite unusuccessful, mules being mules. Out of sight of the lieutenant, we turned left toward Meilu's home, and pulled up five minutes later in her courtyard. Wordlessly, Meilu and Tabitha untied the tarp, removed the newly-loaded case of rum, and handed it to Meilu's grandfather. While they hoisted a case of spring water into the wagon, the grandfather extracted the cork from one of the rum bottles in the Commandante's case, and took a swig.

A smile spread over the old man's face. "Please thank the Commandante for his case of excellent rum!" he said quietly.

Meilu and Tabitha laughed as they secured the tarp over the new case, then nodded to us. Isaiah shook the reins over the mules, and we crawled out of Meilu's courtyard, and resumed our journey to the dock just beyond the Plaza de Armas, where Long John's ship was berthed.

Fifteen minutes later, we plodded onto the dock and stopped before the *Pieces of Eight*. The Commandante and his fat lieutenant marched briskly up as we arrived, the lieutenant setting up a table and producing quill, ink, and paper. Quite a few of Havana's prominent citizens–merchants, ship-owners–seemed to be at the dock, paying much attention to the Commandante. Several fine ladies in brilliant dresses and parasols paraded about.

"Silver! Silver!" the Commandante shouted, looking eager, indeed appearing quite agitated, his eyes darting from the *Pieces of Eight* to the illustrious crowd.

After a moment, Long John appeared at the gangplank, and leisurely hobbled the length of the plank to the dock.

"What do ya want, Commandante?" he said coldly as he arrived at the dock.

"The list of contents of your wagon here, sir, for the payment of duties," the Commandante snapped impatiently. He was so nervous he nearly danced on his toes, shifting his weight constantly from one foot to the other.

Long John took his time, playing the part perfectly.

"Isaiah, Jim. The usual dozen barrels of tobaccy?" he asked.

"Yes, sir," Isaiah answered.

The fat lieutenant was scribbling on a form, which he handed to the Commandante. The Commandante shoved it toward Long John.

"So. Please confirm this as the contents of the wagon for duty purposes." More nervous glances at the crowd of ladies and gentlemen.

Long John studied the paper for a moment, then accepted the freshly dipped quill from the lieutenant, and signed the form.

The Commandante snatched the paper from Long John's hands with a triumphant cry, and held it high as he marched to the back of the wagon, brandishing the paper toward the crowd. He fumbled with the knotted ropes holding the tarp down.

"Lieutenant Sanchez, untie these knots!" he barked hoarsely.

The fat lieutenant hurried over and easily untied the knots. The Commandante shoved him aside and threw back the tarp. The crate was quite visible atop the barrels nestled into the wagon.

A relieved gasp erupted from the Commandante as he saw the crate, followed quickly by a loud, theatrical "Aha!" directed to the crowd. His face beamed.

"Captain Silver, I note a crate of rum bottles in this wagon, which you have failed to register for duty. Smuggling! In the name of the crown of Spain, I arrest you for–"

"Just a moment!" Long John roared. "I disputes that reckless charge!" So saying, he hobbled on his crutch over to the wagon.

"You dispute the existence of this crate you see before you?" the Commandante said with a high laugh, speaking toward the crowd. He reached into the crate and pulled a brown bottle out. "You dispute the existence of these bottles of rum? How dare you!"

Long John calmly hobbled up, and snatched the bottle from the Commandante's hand. He pulled the cork out of the bottle with his teeth, spit the cork onto the dusty ground, and took a long swig, while the Commandante stared goggle-eyed.

"Ahhh," Long John said appreciatively. "That be mighty good, to be sure. But it ain't rum, Commandante. It's water." So saying, he tilted the bottle, and we all watched the clear liquid trickle out and splash over the Commandante's polished boots.

"Careful there, Commandante. Your boots is getting muddy," said Long John.

The Commandante stared at the boots for a long moment, cast an uncomprehending look at Long John, then frantically reached back into the crate and pulled out another bottle. He jerked the cork out and tilted the bottle. More water. Another bottle snatched from the crate–more water. Another, this one smashed against the large wheel of the wagon. More water.

A roar of rage escaped from the poor Commandante as he cast a furious look at Lieutenant Sanchez. The lieutenant stared dumbly back, and slowly scratched his head.

"I believe you owes me an apology, Commandante," Long John said.

"Apology? Apology? You'll get no apology from me, you English dog." He stretched his arm toward Long John. "I arrest you...I arrest you for not declaring a case of water!"

Long John laughed. We heard twitters of laughter from the crowd behind us, which pushed the Commandate to a trembling state of fury.

"Water 'tain't a duty item, you idiot," Long John taunted, stoking the Commandante's fury. "It ain't even required to be listed. You think you can *banish* me from these here *docks* just because I didn't declare water?"

"I do and I will!" the Commandante said in a voice breaking with anger. "Your berth here is reserved for another ship. A Spanish ship, by God. You will vacate it immediately!"

"What?" Long John howled. "As harbormaster, you be required to provide a dockside berth for every merchant ship that requests it. I demands me berth, I do, even if it's–"

"Oh, you shall have your berth, you shall!" the Commandante interrupted in a flash. "You shall have your berth–at the *Guanacaboa* docks!! How does that suit you, Captain Silver?"

Long John paled, and shot a quick glance at me. I was struggling to breathe from shock at the unexpected development, and was quite unable to offer him any help.

"The...Guanacaboa docks?" Long John stammered. "Way at the southern end of the Bay? Why...why..."

The Commandante's face was suddenly beaming, and he nodded his head vigorously, stamping his foot as he darted looks at the astonished crowd behind him. A triumphant smile spread across his face as he took in Long John's obvious confusion and dismay.

Long John's face grew red, and sweat dropped from his chin as he gasped for breath, looking around the dock desperately. The Commandante's pleasure grew as Long John stammered and swayed. My head began to spin, and I thought I would faint.

With a sharp "whack," Long John suddenly struck the dock with his crutch. "Indeed," he proclaimed in a ringing voice. "That be a might hard punishment for not declaring water, Commandante. The Guanacaboa dock adds a half day onto me wagon's journey, over bad roads to boot. But I can stand that. At least ye didn't banish me to the *Del Morro Castle docks*. Oh, that would'a ruined me, by the powers! A full day's wagon ride around the whole bloody bay, over the worst roads ye've ever seen, up and down that steep cliffside trail, wearin' out me mules and me drivers! I guess I can manage it at Guanacaboa, by thunder, and thank me stars ye didn't send me to the Del Morro docks and ruin me."

He hobbled quickly over to Isaiah. "Turn this here wagon 'round and head for Guanacaboa, boys, 'afore the Commandante changes his mind, now. Git going! Hurry!"

"Hold!" roared the Commandante, whose smile had disappeared at Long John's words. He stared hard at Long John.

"I have in fact changed my mind," he shouted, his face half-turned to the crowd, which was buzzing with excitement. "Your berth, Captain Silver, to load your tobacco, is in fact *the Del Morro Castle docks*!"

"No!" bellowed Long John, staggering back a step. "No! Ye can't do that to me, you Spanish pig! It'll be the ruin of me! I can't make a guinea on my tobaccy if it's got to go to that dock!" So saying, Long John raised his crutch and made to lunge at the Commandante. He held back, conveniently, long enough for Isaiah and me to jump from the wagon and restrain him. Once we had him securely held, he struggled a bit more violently.

The Commandante's smile was now completely restored, his face beaming again. He had turned fully to the crowd, and was nodding his head violently, laughter pealing from his mouth.

"The Del Morro docks it is, Silver!" he said in a triumphant tone as he turned back to Long John. "And to show your friend the Governor-General how fair I am, I'll give you extra time, three weeks, to load your crop." He gestured for Lieutenant Sanchez to gather up the table, turned from the struggling Silver, and walked slowly away, toward the crowd. Men there clapped him on the back as he strutted among them, while ladies simpered at his presence, their fans strumming the air.

"No! Ye cain't do this to me, you scum! Not the Del Morro dock!" Long John roared at his back. He shook his fist at the Commander. "No! You've ruined me! Anything but the Del Morro docks!"

By this time the Commandante was laughing loudly, and his stride became positively jaunty. He was accepting congratulations right and left, re-playing his brandishing of the duty papers for all, dramatically ripping away the tarp covering the wagon with a flourish again and again for the ladies' enjoyment.

Isaiah and I looked at Long John, and saw that he was about to burst into laughter himself. We hustled him up the gangplank before he ruined everything. But at the top, as he stepped onto the *Pieces of Eight*, Long John broke away from our grip and leaned over the bulwarks toward the retreating Commandante.

"Ye've ruined me, you Spanish scum!" Long John bellowed, with a mighty shake of his fist. He then turned, and we hurried him to his cabin below decks, where we all three collapsed onto the floor in laughter and, in truth, at relief that the old buccaneer had snatched victory from the jaws of utter defeat. We laughed until we had exhausted ourselves, laughed some more, and lay pleasantly limp and gasping on the floor of the cabin for some time. Long John crawled along the floor on his hands and one knee to where he had flung his crutch, dragged himself up to the table, and took a long swig of rum straight from the bottle there.

"Drink up, me hearties," he roared, suddenly revitalized. "And after that, we'll sail to the Del Morro Castle dock and begin loading our cargo!" Another long swig of rum, then he burst into song, swaying on his crutch.

Fifteen men on the dead man's chest,
Drink and the devil had done for the rest!
Yo ho ho and a bottle of rum!
But one man of her crew alive,
What put to sea with seventy five!
Yo ho ho and a bottle of rum!

Chapter Eighteen. We Load Chinese Treasure

Not wanting to give the Commandante reason to reconsider his decision, Long John vacated the city dock quickly, and promptly sailed across the bay to the Del Morro Castle docks, where he set up residence. By the same thinking, we daren't unload the tobacco barrels at the city docks, so Isaiah and I laboriously made the wagon trip around the bay to the Del Morro docks, which took us fully the rest of the day. Long John was right. The road was horrible–muddy, rutted, and very long. The mules nearly revolted halfway up the long climb to the top of the Del Morro bluff. Then Isaiah nearly revolted as we approached the gate to the Del Morro Castle.

"I can't look, Jim. You take over the reins," Isaiah said with a shudder as we neared the castle gate. Isaiah huddled on the floorboard, trembling, as I drove past the entrance, a huge stone arch bristling with irons bars and soldiers, beyond the wooden bridge over the dry moat. I remembered Long John mentioning how he had purchased Isaiah from the Castle, where he'd been imprisoned for some crime or t'other.

"Is it really that bad in there?" I whispered down to Isaiah as we rumbled past the gate.

Isaiah could only nod.

"We're past it, now," I said.

Isaiah didn't move. "Let me know when we're round the bend and out of sight of it," he whispered up. His face was wet with sweat, and his breathing came quick.

In a few minutes we rounded the corner of the castle. To our right, the upper rampart stretched down the bay side of the castle, filled with soldiers and cannon. Ahead, the road zig-zagged down the steep cliff face in a series of switchbacks. Isaiah took over the reins, and put me on the brake.

The mules liked the steep downhill even less than the previous uphill, mainly because they had a very poor brakeman for the trip. Halfway down, the lower rampart took off to our right, a wide terrace filled with the big cannons called "The Twelve Apostles" and, beyond them, nearly to the sea end of the rampart, the huge gear wheel which operated the chain across the harbor mouth. The mules, the driver, and the brakeman were in a very bad mood by the time we had lurched our way to the dock at the bottom of the road. But there sat the *Pieces of Eight*, and we were greeted by Long John, Meilu, and Tabitha as we limped onto the rough wood planks of the dock.

"Good trip, lads?" Long John asked with a laugh.

We glared at him, red-eyed and covered with dust and sweat.

"Isaiah, 'afore ye take a well-deserved rest, have the crew unload the dozen barrels onto the dock, and leave 'em sitting there. Then get two of your crew to give the mules the water and hay I've got on board, rest 'em four hours, then have the boys start the trip back to Vinales Valley for more tobaccy. I've got three wagons on the way here, ought to arrive tomorrow, do the same routine with them."

Long John turned to me as Isaiah set to his duties. "Jim boy, ye've got two hours 'afore low tide. That gives you an hour of rest, then we four 'uns take off in the longboats for the sea cave and our first load of treasure. Can ye manage that, lad?"

I groaned. "I can manage, but it's highly likely your wagon brakeman's arms will fall off soon. Can I have the cot in your cabin to rest?"

"Aye, and we'll give you some quiet, to boot. Grab a sandwich in the galley on your way there. Go to it, boy."

Food and a bit of a rest went a long way to reviving me. The prospect of claiming Chinese treasure and getting it to the *Pieces of Eight* more than completed the restoration of my strength and spirits. In an hour I was locking my oar in a longboat beside the dock, with Long John on the other oar. Meilu and Tabitha were in the other longboat. Each boat had two empty hogshead barrels in it, one fore and one aft. It turned out that eight of the dozen big barrels in the wagon were in fact empty. Long John had already thought things through.

"Hug the cliff-line, so we're invisible to the Castle," Meilu reminded us. "And don't you two pirates dawdle," she said with a pretend glare.

Indeed, Long John and I were hard-pressed to keep up with the two girls. They were some thirty yards ahead of us by the time they passed out of the mouth of the bay and turned the corner into the open sea, and fifty yards ahead by the time we saw their boat disappear into the opening of the sea cave.

By the time we slid through the opening ourselves–which was thankfully plenty wide, it being just before low tide–their longboat was tied up at a sandy landing in the cavern, and Meilu was just finishing up knocking her head three times on the rocky floor in front of the altar to the sea-goddess *Ma Tsu*, where incense and a candle were burning. I knew Long John shared my opinion of the mysterious black-faced lady sitting larger than life on the altar. We weren't sure who she was, or whether she had any influence, but we knew straight-on that we needed all the luck we could possibly get to pull this off, and we were happy to have Meilu keeping us on the lady's good side.

Long John's eyes fixed on the large golden flask in the center of the altar. It stood nearly a foot high, and appeared to have a stopper atop it, as if it were holding something.

"What be in that chunk of gold there, me lass?" he asked Meilu, as she rose.

Meilu revently took the goblet in her hands. It seemed heavy, by the way she held it. She rotated it back and forth. "Something liquid inside it," she commented, a puzzled look on her face. "There's an inscription. Bring a lantern close."

Eager hands brought lanterns to the altar.

Meilu read the inscription. "*Life is splendid, throwing off bright rays of joy and sorrow, beauty and ugliness, light and dark, in the dance of being. Accept it all. Not wishing to change the flow of the Tao, we may yet wish to respectfully prolong our days of the dance. This elixir invigorates the ch'i and maintains the balance of yin and yang, so your days are without number and the dance stretches far into the unseen future. Long life!"*

Our eyes grew wide.

"Intriguin'," said Long John in a whisper. "Might intriguin'. I don't understand it, but I likes what I hear. Is this–elixir?–the jealous possession of the goddess, or might we take it into our hands?"

Meilu glanced up at the goddess, whose black face and mother of pearl eyes gazed back impassively, with the serenity of eternity.

"She has no need of an elixir–she's already immortal."

"So we may take it from the lady–respectful-like?"

Meilu shrugged, and nodded. She handed the flask to Long John. His eyes greedily studied the golden surface, as he hefted the goblet.

"And might pretty it be, I'm sure," was his verdict. He slipped it into the large inside pocket of his great coat, and fastened the button over the opening.

"This we'll ponder at our leisure, me lads and lasses. Meanwhile, we've work to do."

Tabitha helped us unload our two barrels from the longboat, which she stacked next to theirs in the open space in front of the altar. We had the tops off the barrels soon enough, and Meilu carried over a lacquer chest, this one brimming with porcelain.

"Each chest's contents are already arranged and packed with silk to prevent breakage," she pointed out to us. "All we have to do is close and latch the lid"–doing so as she spoke, an ingenious ivory latch–"then lower the chest into the barrel."

We were all relieved to see the lacquer chest fit nicely into the barrel, laying flat with room to spare all around. Tabitha brought up two more chests, these of jade and ivory, already closed, and we put them atop the first.

"Room for a fourth, I believe," said Meilu. The fourth chest just came up to the top of the barrel. "Perfect," she concluded.

"The ride back will be rough in the rowboat," observed Tabitha. "The chests will shift and slide inside the barrels. They should be wedged in tighter."

We all stared in the barrel, seeing she was right.

I looked at a chest of silk beside me.

"Well, we've got packing material handy right here," I said, lifting the bolts of silk out of the chest, and pushing them into the empty spaces inside the barrel. "Any objections?"

"These here barrels is darn near water-tight," Long John said.

"Even so, let's try not to let you pirates dump a barrel into the water accidentally," Meilu said, grabbing more rolls of silk and filling in the barrel until everything was nicely stuffed.

It didn't take long to pack up our four barrels and fill in the extra spaces with silk. With a final reminder from Meilu to stick close to the face of the cliff and not to dump a barrel overboard–by this time, I was getting pretty tired of her reminders–we set out. The sea seemed rougher on the way back to me, but maybe my arms were just more tired. There was quite a bit of splashing of waves into the boat and onto the barrels, but they were plenty tight to keep the contents dry.

As before, the two girls outstripped Long John and me, which was aggravating, on top of my sore arms. By the time we were into the mouth of the bay, the girls were halfway back to the ship. Their two barrels were already onto the dock, and two more of the empty barrels into their longboat by the time we arrived.

"Looks like a bit over an hour for the whole trip," Meilu called out as they rowed past us for another trip. "We can get one more load before we lose the entrance to the tide," she added cheerily.

I groaned. But after Isaiah had unloaded our first two barrels onto the dock, and loaded us two fresh empty ones, Long John and I dutifully locked oars and began our second trip. The girls had their two barrels loaded by the time we arrived at the sea cave, and were good enough to help us load our two. The water level was appreciably higher on our second exit through the opening to the sea cave, and clearly a third trip was not going to be possible, which was plenty fine with me. Another choppy, wet trip back, and by the time we reached the Del Morro dock, I figured my arms were going to fall off my shoulders in another ten seconds.

"Long John," I said as Isaiah helped us hoist our barrels onto the dock. "You did double duty on the way back this time. Sorry I was so useless."

"Nay, lad. Ye helped drive a wagon most o' the way from Vinales Valley today, being the brakeman down a cliff not hours ago. The wonder 'tis your arms is still working at all. Ye've got twelve hours 'til the next low tide, boy. Take the spare cot in me stateroom again–you've earned a good rest."

In truth, seeing those eight barrels from the girls' and our two trips being loaded onto the *Pieces of Eight*–thirty-two lacquer chests of porcelain, ivory, and jade in all, plus a sight of silk inside each barrel–did make me feel right good as I trudged up the gangplank. I grabbed another sandwich from the galley, but only got half of it eaten before I fell asleep. My dreams were full of miniature landscapes carved in jade, of creamy China plates with gold dragons cavorting on them, and roll and after roll of crimson silk emblazoned with bamboo and fluttering cranes. The *Pieces of Eight* gently rocked, and the smell of saltwater filled my nose. *The wind fills my heart as well as the sails. The salt in my blood calls to the salt of the sea, whose answer wraps me in an ancient embrace. I am at home, where I belong, at peace in the mystery of it all.*

Chapter Nineteen. The Commandante's Discovery

So it went for the next four days, two trips at each of the two low tides, day and night, of our two longboats. Except for the barrels getting splashed and wet in the open longboats, there were no problems, other than all of us having very sore arms–even the girls, I was glad to see. At the end of the four days, it looked like we'd loaded not quite half the treasure in the sea cave. Seventy two of the camouflaged hogshead tobacco barrels sat in the hold, filled with 288 of the lacquer chests, plus another forty or so chests worth of the silk we'd used for filling. And we weren't even halfway through our task! Our exhilaration at the vast Chinese treasure in the *Pieces of Eight's* hold put smiles on our faces and merriment in our hearts, matched only by the weariness of our arms, and our constant watch for the Commandante coming down to the dock.

He came, finally, mid-morning on the fifth day, with Lieutenant Sanchez and half a dozen soldiers. Thank goodness we had returned from our first trip to the sea cave earlier in the day. Long John was on deck as they arrived, with the three of us soon listening at the doorway of the passage from Long John's cabin. Some dozen barrels of tobacco–actual tobacco–were on the dock, along with the four treasure barrels we'd recently delivered.

"Top o' the morning to you, Commandante!" Long John said, as if he were trying awfully hard to be friendly and curry favor.

The Commandante grunted, walking amidst the barrels, running his hand over their tops. "Duty forms submitted for all these barrels, Silver?" he snapped.

"As always, Commandante. Lieutenant Sanchez follows me wagons down from the castle every trip, and we fills out your paperwork like clockwork, we do, eh Sanchez?"

The fat lieutenant nodded eagerly with a smile lighting his face–no one was immune to Silver's charm when he turned it on, save the Commandante.

"I don't suppose there be any berths opening up across the bay, Commandante?" asked Long John, with a plaintive tremor in his voice. "The long trip around the bay and all the up and down from the castle is just about wearing out my wagons and my men."

A smile came to the Commandante's oily face. "It's this berth or none, Silver," he said expansively, patting a barrel.

"But Commandante–"

"This berth or none, and no arguments!" snapped the Commandante.

We all three of us below admired Long John's wily reinforcement of the Commandante's assignment of *Pieces of Eight* to this dock.

Long John slapped the rail in pretended anger, which pleased the Commandante no end. He turned to return to the castle.

"What's this? The barrel is wet," the Commandante remarked, half to himself, as he passed one of our recently delivered treasure barrels. "Why is this barrel wet, Silver?"

Long John stared down at him. "Wet, sir?" He made a show of hobbling slowly down the gangplank.

I shot a worried look at Meilu and Tabitha, who were holding their breath, waiting for what Long John would come up with.

Long John arrived at the barrel. "Oh, that!" he said with a laugh. "It rolled off the dock 'afore me boys could get it upright from the wagon. Plunked right down into the bay, it did, where it bobbed like a cork! Took us some doing to get it up here, you may lay to it." He laughed again, not very convincingly, to our ears.

"Ah. Well, your men are blacks, are they not? These things are to be expected from inferior workers, I have found."

Long John bit his tongue, and remained silent.

By this time the three of us had snuck from the passageway onto the deck, where we watched from a gunner's slot in the bulwarks.

The Commandante slowly turned, and wound his way among the barrels on his way to the far end of the dock. He stopped, with a low whistle.

"Silver. There are three other barrels that are wet, here. Can your slaves be that incredibly clumsy, to drop four barrels off the dock?"

Long John said nothing.

"Lieutenant Sanchez," said the Commandante, with a suspicious glance at Long John. "Put your sword to the top of this barrel, the wet one. Let's see exactly what's inside these wet barrels, that makes them so difficult to handle."

Long John shot an alarmed glance back toward the ship, as Sanchez waddled up to the barrel and slipped his sword under the top-most iron ring to pry it up. Meilu and Tabitha tensed beside me, wide-eyed with sudden panic. The Commandante was opening one of the treasure barrels!

Chapter Twenty. Tabitha's Sacrifice

I clutch momma's amulet at my neck with tight fingers. The Commandante's man loosens the top of the treasure barrel. Everything will be lost. I cannot let it happen, cannot allow the Commandante to destroy my friends' plans. Their dreams.

I am wearing my accustomed black clothes, here on the ship. Before Hawkins and Meilu can stop me, I slide to the gangplank. I drop silent and unseen to the dock. Crouch behind the barrels there, and weave my way to within ten feet of the Commandante. So close I smell his perfume, the expensive lilac scent. I stand, and watch his eyes grow wide with shock.

"Hello, Spanish pig," I hiss.

He splutters. He hits the fat lieutenant on the shoulder.

"It's her! The black devil! After her, you fools! After her!"

Shouts and lunges all around me. I easily avoid their clumsy grabs, and dash from the dock up the road toward the castle. Quickly I lure the Commandante and his men off the dock. They are on the road, huffing along behind me. Especially uphill I outrun them easily. I slow, to keep them close and concentrated on me. The Commandante is in the lead. Sword drawn, face contorted with the old look he would give momma, when he was with Mistress Ravenia–hate, and desire, and more that I cannot fathom and do not wish to.

"It's her! It's her!" the Commandante is shouting behind me, to the soldiers above. "Cut her off at the first rampart! Into the road, you fools!"

I turn the corner, and see a dozen soldiers blocking the road in front of me. To the right is a sheer drop to rocks. To the left is the lower rampart. I run straight at the soldiers, see them tense, raise their swords and pistols.

At the last moment I turn left, onto the rampart's broad terrace.

Large cannons loom ahead of me, the Twelve Apostles. I vault over the first, and land on a power keg, crash to the ground. I am up again before the startled soldiers at the gun can grab me. My ankle hurts. Soldiers are behind the second cannon, so I vault it also, avoiding the bucket of cannister shot–nails, short chains, balls–on the far side as I land. Shouts behind me, as my pursuers get close and grow in number. I vault over another cannon, shooting my hand out to knock over its bucket of nails, balls, and chains to slow them down behind me. I see but few soldiers around the cannons ahead, so I veer right behind them, dashing beside the castle wall. My ankle hurts more. Ahead of me are the last few cannons, and then the huge spoked wheel attached to the chain across the harbor. Beyond that–a low wall ending the rampart. The sea is beyond, blue and clean and cool, but several hundreds of feet below me, a death leap.

I glance back–soldiers everywhere behind me. Shouting, grim and running hard, dodging the nails and chains I've scattered.

Suddenly I hit something, hard. My breath leaves my body. The stink of Spaniards overwhelms me. Strong arms are holding me, wrestling me as we fall to the ground. Three soldiers, hidden behind the great wheel of the chain, have me. We roll on the ground. I bite, spit, hit, kick. Just like I saw momma do against the Bantu slaves when they came back for us under the stairs. And I scream. Especially I scream. But I cannot escape their arms. They drag me to my feet, arms and legs pinned, jerking my head back with my hair.

The Commandante arrives in front of me. His face is red, his chest heaving. He leans, exhausted, against the great wheel, his sword jammed into the ground for support. He glares at me, unable to speak amid his great gasping breathes. Soon a crowd of soldiers surrounds us. Their faces are excited, anticipating–what will the Commandante do to me?

Finally he draws himself up before me. The crowd falls silent. He looms above me. His eyes are bloodshot but triumphant. And full of hate.

The Commandante raises his hand not holding his sword, and hits me, hard, in the face. I taste blood.

"You! For much too long you've had undeserved freedom, you black piece of dirt. I don't know how you eluded me so long. Nor how or why in God's heaven you suddenly appear on my own dock. But here you are!"

He stops, to regain his breath. Suddenly his first whips out, and he hits me again.

A murmur of approval from the soldiers. They are hoping for more.

I am silent. He staggers after his second blow, then regains his feet. Looms high above me again. I look up into his face, and spit.

"Aii!!" He staggers back, and wipes the spit off his face. He lifts his sword. The soldiers gasp, then crowd closer.

He breathes very deep. His fingers tighten on the hilt of the sword.

I do not move. Death does not frighten me. I will miss my new friends. But I will be with my momma. And my father.

His sword quivers above me, reflecting sunlight. It is beautiful, silver, glinting against the clouds gathering in the blue sky.

Then it slowly drops. Back to his side.

"No." He shakes his head.

"It will not be this quick, when I kill you," he says. "No. It will be slow. And very painful, for you."

He grabs me by the hair. The soldiers fall away. "Stay close, in case she wrestles free. She is a demon, this one." He jerks me by my hair, back along the rampart. "I'll personally escort you to the dungeon. The far dungeon." He manages a laugh. "We'll play with you for several days, though you won't enjoy it." The soldiers join his laughter.

He pulls my face close to his. His face is sweaty, and smells more of sweat than his fancy lilac perfume.

"I'll torture you, you black devil, for days. Then I'll slit your throat and watch you bleed to death. Slowly."

The soldiers are silent.

Soon I will be with my momma again. And my father. I will see *Obatala*, and kneel before him. And *Chango*, the thunder god, and all the other *orishas.*

He jerks me along by my hair. I stumble after him. My ankle hurts.

Chapter Twenty One. Jim Makes Emergency Plans

I gave Meilu a hand coming off the rigging of the port shrouds. She was shaken, and stiff with fear. We had climbed to the crows nest to see Tabitha's chase along the lower rampart, which was only a little higher than our perch there. Meilu had flinched each time the Commandante hit Tabitha. Our last view of our friend was her being dragged up to the castle behind the Commandante's huge figure, turning the corner and then out of our sight.

In Long John's cabin, now, we sat stone-faced, staring at his desk. Tabitha was in the castle's dungeon, in the power of the Commandante. It seemed a dream. A very bad dream.

"She kept the Commandante from discovering our treasure, she did," Long John finally said. "But what a price to pay, by thunder!"

He took a swig of rum, and pushed the bottle to me. I didn't touch it.

"The Commandante isn't stupid," I observed. "In time, he'll remember about the barrels. And wonder why Tabitha showed up beside our ship, of all places."

"Aye," Long John growled, taking another swig of the rum. "Aye, I reckon he'll be occupied with Tabitha the rest of today, but bring us to mind tomorrow."

"Which means we've got to be gone tonight," I stated. "Before they raise the chain across the harbor mouth at sunset, we've got to be on the far side of it."

Meilu roused herself from her stupor.

"I'm not leaving without Tabitha," she said in a hoarse voice.

"What?" Long John said. "Put Tabitha out of your mind, girl. She's dead."

"Not yet, she's not," Meilu spit back, suddenly alive again, tears welling in her eyes. "And she's my friend. She's my sister." She burst into sobs, but quickly shoved them away. "I'm not leaving without her," she repeated in a broken but determined voice. "If it's her dead body I take back, then so be it."

She rose, as if to take off then and there for the castle.

"Whoa, my determined filly," Long John said, putting a large hand on her arm. "Ye'll simply get yourself killed in the bargain if ye go charging up to the castle just like that."

"I'm going into the castle to rescue her," Meilu said flatly. "Today. Now. Before...before too much can happen to her."

"Aye, and that's a fine thing to want to do," said Long John. "And you be right about one thing–the Commandante won't kill her right off. No, he'll want to have his fun with her for awhile, you may lay to that."

"Meilu," I interrupted. "You do realize–if you go into the castle, you're not likely to come out alive."

Meilu nodded. "She would do the same for me. She did in fact go on the Black Pan junk with me. I must go to her."

Silence.

"Do ye even have your little throwing weapon with you, dearie?" Long John asked.

She cried aloud in frustration. "It's back at my home! How stupid, *stupid* of me!" she wailed. "But I'm not taking the time to go get it. I'm leaving. Soon. Even without any weapons."

I marveled at her courage. Or foolishness. I desperately wanted to help her on her impossible quest.

"You are not without weapons," I found myself saying. I touched her temple. "Your mind is a weapon, your best weapon." I touched her arm, above the elbow where the big muscle shows. "And you have strength here, also."

I bent down to my calf, where I had taken to carrying a dirk of my own, strapped in a case. I untied the strap, then made bold to shove her pant leg up high enough to strap the case and its dirk onto her own calf. Her leg was warm to my touch. Soft, but firm.

"There. Another weapon. A silent one. Should you need it." I grinned at her. "You're bristling with weapons, China girl."

She seemed confused. Dazed. Why would she be so dazed? It must be that the enormity and long odds of what she was about to attempt had finally dawned on her.

"Isaiah!" Long John shouted. To our puzzled looks, he said, "The boy's been in the dungeon of the castle. He'll be able to draw a map of the route, for Meilu. That'll increase the odds of our seeing you again–though not much, I be feared."

Isaiah appeared at the door, as Meilu took a few steps to test the feel of my dirk against her calf.

"Meilu's might determined to get into the castle and try to rescue Tabitha," Long John said to him. "Today."

Isaiah gasped.

"Yes, I know. But she's bound to try. Take the parchment, quill, and ink from the desk here, and huddle with Meilu in her and Tabitha's room. Draw her some maps and diagrams–whatever'll help her get to the dungeons."

"And back," I added firmly.

"Aye, and back," Long John agreed. "Isaiah–I imagines they takes their siesta in the castle, same as Spaniards everywhere?"

Isaiah, wide-eyed and trembling at the prospect of even thinking about the castle and its dungeons, nodded.

"Then I suggest you two get at it," said Long John, nodding to Meilu. "Ye've got an hour or so 'afore they're into their siestas. Learn the layout of the place. Come up with a plan." He stared up at the ceiling, thinking. "Jim and me'll drive ya in our wagon up the road, have some trouble right in front of the gate, and ye'll slip out of the back of the wagon and into the castle–somehow."

Meilu rose, grabbed the parchment, quill and ink from the desk, and hurried out of the room. Isaiah followed her down the passageway.

Long John stared soberly at me. "This'un makes rescuing her grandfather from the Black Pan and his Arab look simple, ya realize that?"

I nodded. We both knew it wasn't likely Meilu would come back from the castle. I felt like I was going to throw up. I stood, shook my head, and tried to think of us and our own plight. It seemed easier than thinking of Meilu and Tabitha.

"Long John–you know the Commandante and his men could come back here to the dock sooner, rather than later," I said.

"Aye, we'd best be ready to be off in an instant," he agreed, rising and grabbing his crutch. "And at most, as ye rightly point out, we've got to be on the other side of that chain a'fore sunset today."

"But while we wait for the siesta, and Meilu and Isaiah are going over the layout of the castle, I want to take a longboat to the sea cave," I said.

Long John stared at me as if I were mad, then collapsed into his chair again. "By thunder, Jim Hawkins, why in tarnation would ye want to do that?"

"Because I can't bear the thought of the Commandante finding out about the cave and plundering it," I answered. "You and I know it's likely that he's going to have two prisoners instead of one at the end of this day. And he's already come pretty close to discovering a barrel full of Chinese treasure. If he convinces either Tabitha or Meilu to tell him where the treasure is–"

"Aye, he has his ways, he has. I understand he has a man in that deep dungeon that could make a deaf mute sing like a canary."

"Exactly. I'm not going to let the Commandante row into that sea cave. It wouldn't be right–not even to let him *look* at the black-faced sea-goddess there, much less get his dirty hands on her and all her treasure."

"Why, Jim Hawkins. I didn't realize you was so all-fired sentymental-like."

"Well, so what?" I bristled. "Look, I've been studying that square stone atop the entrance to the sea cave, Long John, these past four days. I think you're right–it was put there, by the Chinese. If they can put it there, I can get it out. And without that stone to mark the entrance, especially if you aren't looking at low tide, why, the sea cave will be invisible."

"And maybe invisible to us, my lad," Long John said, peevishly.

"So?"

"So I'm having some difficulty, me boy, at the prospect of giving up all that treasure still in the cave."

That made me angry. I leaped up and thrust my face into his. "Long John, even with less than half of it on the *Pieces of Eight*, we've got more treasure here than any of the four of us can spend in a lifetime," I shouted in his face. "Don't be greedy, you bloody pirate!"

He glared at me for a long moment, then slapped the table with his palm and laughed.

"By thunder, I likes the way you talks to me, Jim Hawkins," he roared. "Ye sound like me missus, sometimes, and that's not a bad thing. Take your blame longboat. But what if we have some excitement here while you're gone?"

"If I'm close to arriving back, I'll be a flank attack on the Commandante. If I'm still out in the sea, then you just pick me up as you sail out."

"Aye, assuming they haven't yanked that great hulkin' chain up early," Long John said, wheeling toward the door on his crutch. "Ye've got your pistol, boy?"

I touched it, under my vest, as we hurried up the passageway to the stairs. "Here, take me dirk–ye've given your own away, and it makes me nervous, it does, sendin' ye off without one." I accepted his old battered knife as we reached the top of the stairs.

"All hands, listen up," Long John roared as we emerged into the open air. His crew came rushing to the poop deck where we stood.

"Me lads, we be in some trouble with the Commandante. Pity, eh?"

A chorus of laughs from the men. Their dark faces glowed, eager for a fight.

"From here on out, ever'thing's on an urgent schedule, me lads. If'n anyone sees the Commandante and a gaggle of his soldiers approaching the dock, we need to hear from ya, and we need to be off in a rush. Isaiah's busy, so Ned, you're in charge, right?"

"Yes, sir!" said a lanky fellow, stepping front and center.

"Listen up, all of you. Ned here will see to it all this gets done, and might quick. We needs four men stand'n ready to weigh anchor quicker'n you can swig a tankard of rum. At the same time, I want half a dozen on the yardarms, ready to furl the sails in the same time." Long John scanned the skies. "There's precious little breeze now, though it feels and smells like a storm's coming. If it's not here when we need to be off, then we'll need every scrap of canvas to help this puny breeze push us over that bloody chain and out of the bay. And come hell or high waters, we're dead set to be out of this here bay 'afore sunset tonight, lads!"

His voice rising, Long John continued. "The rest of you load those four wet barrels into the hold, then move the remaining barrels against the side of the ship, as barricades. We'll probably be taking some lead from the Commandante and his men, and those barrels will stop the shots 'afore they hurt me precious *Pieces of Eight*."

The men stared, spellbound, at Long John as he hobbled along the poop deck, bellowing orders. "Men, can ya warm to the notion of a battle with the Commandante and his soldiers?"

A great answering roar from the crowd of eager faces.

"Then when ye've got the barrels in place and everything done, those not on the yardarms and the anchor grab a musket apiece from the galley. Prime 'em good, men! Dry power and heavy shot! I have a feeling we'll be killing some Spaniards today!"

With another roar the men gathered around Ned and soon were dashing off on his orders.

I ran to the gangplank and looked back at Silver on the poop deck. "I'm off for the sea cave, Captain Silver! You're sounding like a pirate captain, Long John!"

The big one-legged man threw back his head and laughed loud. "Aye, lad, and I'm feeling like a pirate captain! I'm feeling like killing Spaniards and busting out of this here bay and headin' for the open seas. Me own course, lad! Me own schedule, lad! The wind in me sails and salt smell in me nose!"

"*Yo ho ho and a bottle of rum!*" I shouted back at him, then jumped to the dock and dashed for the longboat, liking the feel of the wood on my bare feet.

Chapter Twenty Two. Saying Goodbye to the Sea Goddess

The tide was just beyond its highest, and beginning to run out of the bay, so even rowing the longboat alone, I made good time through the mouth to the open sea. I reflected that the same tide would help push the *Pieces of Eight* out of the bay. We'd need every bit of help we could get, given the muggy, still air. I glanced up at the gathering clouds.

While rowing, I thought of Tabitha, somewhere deep inside the fortress, wherever the dungeons were. And of Meilu, about to join her there. It was too horrible to think of, and made my throat tight and achey, so I put it out of my mind and concentrated on the rowing.

Soon I was in front of the entrance to the sea cave, or what was left of it at the nearly high tide. Thanks to the tide, the square stone marking the entrance was at eye level for me. It was about a foot square, and fashioned from the same type of stone as the cliff face–visible more for sticking out from the cliff, and throwing a shadow, than anything else. In the lull between waves, I had a good purchase on the stone, and tried pulling it out toward me, hoping it would slide easily. It didn't. I took Long John's old pirate dirk out of my belt, and tried prying the stone out. While I could get the point of the dirk between the stone and the cliff, the stone didn't want to move regardless of the pressure I applied to pop it out toward me. I tried all four sides–no luck. Finally I leaned on the blade with such pressure that the tip of the dirk broke off. Long John wouldn't like that.

Arms aching, and frustrated, I sat down in the longboat and looked up at the square stone. It just wouldn't come out. Maybe I could just break it up. I rowed right against the cliff face, lifted one of the oars, and hit the rock from the side. No luck. Hit it again, and again, from underneath, and above. It was too hard by far for the oar and my faltering blows. I sat down again, nearly in tears. The thought of the Commandante and his men swarming around *Ma Tsu's* altar inside, shouting and laughing as they looted the Chinese treasure, haunted me. I could not let that happen. Yet there was the marking stone, plain as day, sticking out from the cliff face, in spite of all my efforts.

I stared at it. And wondered. I had been exerting all my efforts to pull the stone *out*. It was the same material as the rest of the cliff. What if there were a space behind it, and I could push it *in*? If it were level with the cliff around it, and throwing no shadow, it would blend in. I rowed to directly in front of the stone, waited for a lull between waves, and stood in the longboat. Taking the oar in my hands again, I held it like a whaler holds a harpoon. I lined the end of it up carefully, and plunged it against the center of the stone.

I stumbled at the force of oar against stone, and fell into the bottom of the longboat. I scrambled to my feet, and examined the stone. Yes! It had sunk in, maybe an inch or two of the six inches it stuck out! I picked up the oar again, rowed the longboat close, and waited for the next lull. Stood before the stone, oar raised like a harpoon again. When the lull arrived, I steadied myself, and rammed the end of the oar into the center of the stone again, throwing all my weight into it. The stone plunged all the way into the cliff this time, finishing up level and unnoticeable.

As I was staring at it, astonished and elated, the cliff began to rumble and shake. The sound built, and great splashes erupted in the little entrance left at the high tide, until suddenly the longboat was shoved away from the entrance by an enormous wave that roared out of it, knocking me off my feet and, indeed, out of the boat altogether. Spluttering and wild with fear, I reached out and grabbed the bowline as it whipped past me. I was dragged some dozen yards away from the cliff by the fierce current. Spitting water and eyes smarting from the salt, I pulled myself along the bowline and to the bow of the boat, which was bucking in the current. I gathered my strength, and pulled myself up into the longboat.

My eyes quickly went to the cliff. There, just below the nearly invisible marker stone, foam was still issuing from a great pile of rocks blocking the former entrance. More stones dropped down onto the top of the pile as I looked. The sea cave entrance was filled with stones–blocked forever, by the cunning of the Chinese three hundred years ago. Long John would have cried, but I was glad. *Ma Tsu* and her beautiful treasures were safe.

Wearily I locked the oars, and pulled away. Looking back after half a dozen strokes, the stone marker and the former entrance were invisible, even to me. With a strange feeling in my heart, part sadness and part elation, I resumed my rowing. And wondered what I would find transpiring in the bay. With luck, I'd be able to see Meilu off in her dreadful journey into the fortress.

* * * *

She waited for the turbulence to subside, the echoes of the crashing rocks and waves surging from one side of the cave to the other, even the air overwhelmed by the thundering noise and energy. Finally it all subsided into the black silence from which it had so suddenly emerged. She knew that it would be far longer than three centuries until the next disturbance. Her little cave was now in the firm embrace of the promontory, a small bubble in a mountain of rock. That was fine. She had patience, overflowed with patience, even patience to endure until the great mother Chaos engulfed all and began anew the immense Cycle. The millennia were nothing to her. The ch'i of the rock all around her was pleasant, slow and deep, perfectly attuned to the path of the Tao. The ch'i of the sea, of course, reached in still, between the spaces in the great mound of stones, reminding her of her own origin. But it was the ch'i of the contents of the surrounding lacquer chests that warmed her. The delicate, subtle, pure pulse of silk and jade and porcelain, overlain with the artisan-created patterns of mountains, birds, lakes, insects, streams, fish, trees, clouds. Ah, yes. Plenty to enjoy for an eternity here! She settled into herself, briefly wondering what would become of the four recent intruders. Yet they passed quickly from her attention. They were but a brief ripple on the wave of eternity, and whatever happened to them was right and would join with all the other pulses of energy to constitute the vast pattern of all that was, the great Tao of being that was right and good and beyond questioning or wondering about. She stared into the darkness, immersed in the Tao and reveling in it with the stately rhythm of the ages.

Chapter Twenty Three. Meilu into the Dungeons

It comforted me to hear from Hawkins that he had sealed my *Ma Tsu* and her remaining treasures in the sea cave from the Commandante and his men. Only I knew how much I needed some comfort. Though I pretended calm and confidence, I was shaking with fear as I crouched in the back of the wagon Hawkins and Silver were driving up the winding road to the gate of the castle. I was covered with the tarp and wearing Tabitha's dark clothing, but felt very conspicuous.

No matter. Tabitha was in the castle's dungeon. She was a sister to me, now. We were two caterpillars, in our chrysalis time, struggling to emerge into–what? Neither of us knew. But both of us had committed to accompany the other on the strange journey. I could no more leave Tabitha in the castle dungeon than she could leave me on the Black Pan ship.

Isaiah's map of the castle's interior was burned into my mind. My route to the dungeons–and the danger points getting there–were clear to me. We were well into the siesta time, so navigating unseen inside the castle was not impossible to imagine. Getting past the guards at the castle entrance was going to be more difficult. For that, I had to trust to Silver and Hawkins.

I tried to let my fear bubble up and out of my mind. I also tried to jettison the dazed feeling that had overwhelmed me as Hawkins had touched my leg in Silver's cabin. I didn't understand why his touch affected me so. Nothing like that had ever happened to me before.

Later. Later I would try to figure it out. Now I was in the back of a wagon approaching the infamous Castillo del Morro, a dirk strapped to my calf. The route to the castle's dungeon–and my sister Tabitha–burned into my mind. Nothing else existed. Nothing else mattered.

We turned the last corner of the road, and approached the intersection with the drawbridge over the castle's dry moat, on the left. Beyond the drawbridge, the stone arch of the gate loomed dark, two guards slouching against the wall in the gloom. I liked how dark it was there. Already, I was thinking like my sister.

As Silver had instructed me, I shoved a barrel out the back of the wagon at the far end of the drawbridge. The barrel rolled a few turns, and stopped just in front of the bridge.

"Whoa!" Silver roared to the mules, pulling on the reins and bringing the wagon to a halt. "By thunder, what in tarnation's got into you, you knuckle-headed young idiot," he bellowed at poor Hawkins beside him. "I told ya to tie that barrel down, ya numbskull of a dog's whelp! Lookit the thing!"

Silver laboriously lowered himself to the ground as Hawkins dashed over to the barrel and made a show of shoving it, to no avail. Silver was holding a large flagon of rum in each hand now, and he elaborately took a long swig of each, waving them in plain view of the guards, whose attention he had completely.

"Lift that barrel back onto the wagon, you miserable excuse for a servant," he roared at Hawkins, who seemed quite incapable of even rolling the barrel, much less lifting it single-handedly back into the wagon.

"Avast, ye young whelp! You're as weak as a pup!" Silver roared. He looked over to the guards, who had emerged from the shadows to watch Silver berate the boy.

"You there! You looks thirsty, ye do. Come have a swig of this fine Jamaican rum to limber ye muscles, then help me boy load this barrel!" He waved the rum flagons toward the guards.

For their part, the guards looked at each other, then at the rum flagons, then back into the gloom of the entry. Not seeing their commanding officer–who was doubtless asleep–they edged onto the drawbridge toward the wagon.

As they did so, the feverishly grunting Hawkins finally managed to roll the barrel, but apparently in the wrong direction, toward the mules at the front of the wagon, rather than toward the back. The barrel came to a halt against the front wheel of the wagon.

"Tarnation, boy, what are ye doing? Ye're going the wrong way! Good thing these excellent Spaniards are a'coming to help us." He waved the rum toward the guards again, as he moved to the front of the wagon beside the barrel. He reached his arms out, and offered a flagon to each of the guards, which had a wondrously immediate effect of convincing them to quickly lurch across the last of the drawbridge and up to the wagon.

My cue. As they arrived at the front of the wagon and eagerly swigged the rum, I slipped under the tarp at the back end of the wagon, dropped to the ground on bare feet, and like a shadow flitted to the drawbridge, and was across it and into the dark gateway before they finished their swallows.

Reaching the stone wall, I pressed against it and hesitated briefly, to allow my eyes to adjust to the gloom. My heart was beating wildly. I checked my right leg to confirm that Hawkin's dirk was still strapped securely there. Then I plunged under the arch and into the castle, hugging the dark stone walls. The cavernous entry hall was before me, circular, as Isaiah said it would be. The far left passageway out of it led to the arsenal, and past that the dungeons. The quickest route was straight through the middle of the deserted hall. But I kept to my plan, and skirted its curved outer wall, staying in the shadows. I moved quickly and silently.

Just as I approached the passageway, a soldier emerged out of it, rubbing his eyes sleepily. I froze, as he passed not a yard in front of me. He continued on, disappearing into the guardhouse at the far end of the hall. I peeked my head cautiously around the corner, into the passageway.

Clear.

I dash down the passageway, counting openings on the left. At the fifth, I pause. Stairs lead down. That is the direction I want to go. But Isaiah had said that the sixth opening was the stairs to the dungeon. I freeze, paralyzed with indecision. Then quickly follow the passageway further, to the sixth opening. It is level. I advance some six feet into it–no stairs. I dash back to the opening, and slink back along the passageway to the fifth opening.

Ma Tsu, help me. I don't know what to do. But I know I must go down, and here are stairs. Guide my feet, Ma Tsu.

I take a deep breath, and race down the stairs. They descend in a spiral, past doors on each side. Just as Isaiah said they would. I feel better. At a landing, a door opens, and a soldier stumbles out, turning to close the door behind him. I freeze and press into the wall. He turns, and walks half past me before he notices me. His eyes widen, and he stares, puzzled, directly at me.

The dirk is in my hands, and I plunge it deep into his belly before he can move or cry out. I don't mean to, it just happens, a thing that must be done. He crumples against me with a surprised gurgle. I feel his warm blood on my shirt. I edge away from his body, and gingerly open the door he came from. A small room, no one else there. I drag his body into the room–it is heavy, but I am strong and in a hurry–and close the door.

Back down the stairs. I don't have time to think about what I've just done. Rescuing my sister is all I can think of. I arrive at the first dungeon level. There is the table, and there the dungeon master asleep with his head on the table, as Isaiah had said he would be, a bottle of rum beside him. And the keys above his head, on the wall behind.

I creep to him, and gently lift the keys. Holding them against my stomach to muffle any noise, I slink to the dark opening at the far end of the landing. Torches on the walls give off flickering light, barely illuminating the rough stone steps falling steeply down. I nearly slip and fall on the first step. It is wet, and covered with something slimy and slippery. Not loosening my grip on the keys pressed against my stomach, I put my other hand against the wall to steady myself, and descend the stairs as quickly as I dare.

The air is very bad, foul and reeking with the smell of burning tar, slime on the stairs, and Spanish sweat. It is cold down here, colder than I have been since my winter in China last year. I hurry on, getting the feel of the slippery stairs. It seems like I've been climbing down these stairs forever. I realize I'm slowing down, not wanting to go further into the dimly lit gloom, the cold, the foul air.

Then I remember.

Tabitha is down here, below me. My sister. I plunge on, quicker. Through more twists and turns. Finally it seems a bit less dark ahead, and I see another platform opening ahead of me. I arrive at the deeper dungeons, and peek cautiously into the platform from the stairway.

What is that? Some things moving, along the floor. I hesitate. Then I hear their squeaks. The floor is alive with rats. I shudder, and step into the area. A scream from my right. I flatten myself against the wall. Soon, a laugh, harsh and rasping. That would be him. The Commandante's man that Silver told me about. The torture expert.

His victim screams again. It is not my sister, thank the gods.

The platform is circular, with small barred windows in wooden doors around the perimeter. I glide to the left and look through the first window. I can see nothing.

"Tabitha!" I hiss through the bars. Wait tensely. Nothing.

To the second window. "Tabitha!" Again nothing.

"Tabitha!" at the third window. Something stirs. A rat?

A soft cry. "Meilu?"

My heart leaps.

"Can you stand? Move?" I whisper through the bars.

"Meilu?" again, unbelievingly.

"Yes!" I snap. "Get ready to leave."

I try the first key on the ring in the heavy iron lock. Twist it to the left, then the right. No. The second key. Again, no.

I jump at another harsh laugh behind me. I whirl around, the dirk quickly in my hand. Nothing. The Spaniard is still in the cell on the other side. I put the dirk back in its case, and try the third key. To the right–nothing. To the left–it clicks, pushes something aside, and the lock is clear!

I shove the door open and slip inside, closing it behind me.

This cell faces the cliff face, and a tiny opening high in the far stone wall lets in a feeble shaft of light, above a crude wooden bed there. Tabitha is staring at me, wild-eyed, as if I am a ghost. Her face is bloody, and swollen. I wrap her in a tender hug. She is crying.

"Meilu. Why? How?" She is stammering, tears flowing down her battered face.

"Quiet. Can you walk? Run?"

She nods. "He's concentrating on my face, for now."

I smile into her eyes, then see them go from relief to shock to terror. I whirl around.

He is huge, larger than the Commandante, filling the door. As big as the Arab was. His naked chest is heavily muscled, his hands the size of hams, and wrapped in leather. But it is his eyes that grab my attention, deep black wells of insanity and cruelty. Tabitha and I back away from him. He laughs, like metal scraping over stone.

"Two to enjoy, now," he grunts in a grating voice. He steps toward us, slow, threatening, enjoying it.

Tabitha and I back to the stone wall. Nowhere else to go. I am numb, nearly paralyzed with terror. I think to grab Hawkin's dirk from my calf, but realize the giant would merely swat it away with those huge leather-gloved hands. Better to keep it in reserve, as a surprise. It is Tabitha who moves. She bends down, tosses a dirty blanket aside, and lifts one of the wooden planks forming the bed. She thrusts it into my hand, then bends to grab another for herself. The planks are about five feet long, but heavy, three inches or so square, of solid wood.

The man stops, then throws back his head and laughs at our puny threat. Roars with laughter. Hits his huge leathery hands against his chest with delight. Still laughing, he steps toward us.

We glance at each other to time our blows, then both swing the planks in wide, opposite arcs at his head, as hard as we can swing them.

He easily catches a plank in each hand and stands there, arms outstretched. He lifts the planks–and us still holding onto them–into the air, and laughs again, eyes shut in the intensity of his merriment.

I drop to the ground, steady my footing quickly, and launch myself full force at his face, my arms stretched to the front, stiff thumbs leading my assault. I aim for his closed eyes, and do my very best to drive each thumb straight through them. I slam into his eyes.

His screams fill the cell, echoing off the walls. He drops the planks and slaps his hands over his agonized eyes, bent over in his pain.

Tabitha and I quickly grab the dropped planks, and I give the first blow, lifting the plank high and bringing it down onto his head with all my strength. The plank shatters, and the giant drops to his knees with a deep gasp. Tabitha's blow comes next, lands at the base of his skull, and sends him flat to the stone floor, his arms outstretched and jerking as he utters low moans. We stare at the huge, writhing mass of muscle against the stones.

I come to my senses first. Slit his throat with the dirk? No. He is immobilized, and I am tired of killing already. I take Tabitha's hand. "Quickly. Follow me." I grab a torch from the wall at the landing as we burst from the cell and scramble up the stairs.

"Careful. The steps are slippery."

We scramble up the stairway, falling often, but always up, flying from the horror behind us. We reach the first dungeon. The guard is stretching and rubbing his eyes at the table. He grunts in surprise as we emerge from the stairs, and lurches to his feet. As he reaches out to block our way, I shove the torch into his face. With a shout he falls backward as we race by and plunge into the next stairway, up to the main castle.

"The prisoner! The black devil! She escapes! She escapes!" we hear him shouting behind us. Scuffling sounds ahead of us, men rousing themselves. I let go of Tabitha's hand and grab the dirk from my calf.

"Take this. We'll see if steel and fire can cut through them up ahead."

Tabitha nods as she accepts the dirk. "Sister. I'm not going back to the dungeon," she states. "I'd rather die in the air than in the dark."

"Well, you're going in the right direction, then," I say, clutching the torch tightly in my hands as it leads our way up the stairs toward the sound of men gathering.

She has called me "sister"! I note it, but am much too busy to appreciate it.

The climb seems to take forever. Finally I see the opening at the top of the stairs, which leads to the passageway from the entrance hall. We burst out of the stairwell into a knot of three soldiers, roused by the shouts from below, who are just strapping on their swords. My torch is in the face of the first one, who falls back with a scream. The second reaches for us, and receives the sharp point of a dirk in his hand from Tabitha. He howls, and the third quickly falls back with him.

I lead Tabitha toward the entrance hall in full flight, exulting that we have broken through. But as we near the hall, a pistol shot echoes sharply through the passage. It doesn't threaten us, but it does alert others ahead of us. I change my tiring grip on the torch, realizing what a poor weapon it is. But we are for fleeing, not for fighting, if we are to have any chance of reaching Silver's ship.

More soldiers as we fly into the large entrance hall, half a dozen maybe, also fresh from siesta. The castle gate beckons at the far end of the circular hall. No pressing against walls this time. Straight through the center of the hall we race, whipping torch and dirk in circles around us. The soldiers are Spaniards–never eager for a fight. They half-heartedly reach for us, but are soon convinced to avoid the fire and the steel of the torch and dirk.

We are out, into the blessed daylight and open air. I hear Tabitha weeping with joy behind me, just to be out of the castle, even as she slashes with the dirk. No time for weeping for me. A guard is on the drawbridge. I knock him into the moat with the torch, and we are on the road toward the dock, lungs bursting, legs trembling from the long, furious climb up from the dungeons. But we are free!

No, not free. The soldiers we have burst through are behind us, pursuing in an angry, shouting crowd, ashamed at having two slim girls bowl them over. Spaniards are not much for battle, but they hate to be shamed. Especially by girls. We flee before them, much faster than they can run, and soon the far corner of the castle is in sight ahead of us, where the road dives toward the docks. Musket balls pepper the road around us, balls of dust erupting at our feet. The soldiers are brave enough to shoot fleeing girls in the back, it appears.

Tabitha trips beside me, and sprawls in the dust. I reach down, scoop her up, and drag her along with me. More musket shots. My shoulder suddenly stings. Blood blooms under my glance. But I can still run. It is only a surface wound. Will we ever make the corner of the castle, to see the ship?

Chapter Twenty Four. Jim to the Crows Nest

Long John and I had added the wagon to the barrels fronting the *Pieces of Eight*. Though we anxiously wondered what was happening to Meilu in the castle, our attention was quickly centered on the Commandante and some fifty men, who appeared on the road not long after our return from the castle.

"To your stations, men!" Long John shouted. "And start weighing that anchor now!" Soon the yardarms were bristling with crew, with more kneeling behind the bulwarks, muskets in hand.

"Silver! You are under arrest," bellowed the Commandante, who was standing safely behind the large figure of Lieutenant Sanchez as he reached mid-dock.

"Be I smuggling more of your precious water, Commandante?" Long John returned.

"Whatever is in those wet barrels, I am confident it is contraband," the Commandante screeched in his high voice. "Moreover, I am convinced you have been harboring the runaway slave girl. You tried to disguise her, and nearly had me fooled. But you cannot fool the Commandante!"

"Oh, you're a sharp one, you are," Long John taunted. "For a Spaniard, that is. You're as sharp as a sword that's been cutting turtle shells for a week, that you are."

"No more words, you English dog. Will you surrender?"

"Lads, give him our answer!"

Sails suddenly bloomed from the yardarms of the two masts, and musket shots exploded from the bulwarks. Half a dozen of the soldiers fell where they stood, as the Commandante and the rest stumbled over each other frantically falling back to the edge of the dock, where they quickly ducked behind boulders and posts.

I had imagined the *Pieces of Eight* majestically sailing away from the dock, but in fact the breeze was so slight that our movement was more of snails than swans, even with full sail. But as the soldiers returned our fire, we at least were inching away from the dock, pushed more by the outgoing tide than any wind.

"I'll have your head for this, Silver!" the Commandante yelled from behind a post. "Return your ship to the dock, I order you." The dock was soon engulfed in smoke from the musket shots whizzing in both directions.

"I be trembling in me boots, Commandante!" roared Long John through the smoke. "Trim them sails, me lads. Isaiah, keep us close to the cliff face, and take us to the mouth of this here bay."

"Return to the dock!" roared the Commandante.

"Join me for a rum at Kingston!" roared Long John back. "And quit hiding behind your fat lieutenant, you cowardly Spaniard, so I can put a shot through your fancy uniform!"

We could hear Lieutenant Sanchez's hurt howl at Long John's mention of him, then his voice came. "Commandante! They're sailing away!"

"Ha! Sailing? More like rowing. We'll have the chain up and them bottled in like pigs in a slaughterhouse before they're halfway to the mouth."

Through the smoke, we could see the Commandante's large figure emerge from behind the post. "Blue platoon–stay here, pour fire into them. Red platoon–with me and Sanchez, up the road to the first rampart. Shout ahead to raise the chain and prime the Twelve Apostles. We'll bottle them in, and blast them to their English hell! Ha, ha!" His high-pitched laugh echoed over the dock.

"Aargghhh!" Long John bellowed into the smoke. "I'd give me other leg for a good stiff breeze! Where is this misbegotten storm that be threatening all day?"

Indeed, as the Commandante and half his men rushed up the road toward the first rampart, I knew he was right–the chain would bottle us up inside the harbor and the Twelve Apostles would blow us to smithereens. With a sick feeling, I realized that we were just as bad off as Tabitha and Meilu.

I heard shots, then, from further off. Higher. My eyes rose to the top of the road, where it swung around the corner of the castle. Meilu and Tabitha came tearing around the corner, torch and dirk slashing in all directions, holding a pursuing mob of half-hearted soldiers at bay. They soon turned and flat-out ran down the road, towards us.

"Long John! Meilu and Tabitha are coming down the road!"

"And so are the Commandante and a score of soldiers, going up!" Long John despaired. "They won't fight through that many." His eyes gauged the road. "They'll meet at the first rampart, and be forced onto it, like Tabitha was before. Jim lad, up to the crows nest. You'll have the view, there. Let me know what happens on the rampart!"

I scurried to the port shrouds, sick with despair but wanting, like Long John, to be able to see what transpired on the rampart. I was quickly onto the rigging.

"And take this, me boy, in case some soldiers take potshots at ya up there, exposed as ya be."

I saw a musket flying through the air toward me from Long John's hand. I caught it smartly, slung it across my back by the strap, and clambered up the rigging. I'd be nearly at the rampart's level in the crows nest, and I was already dreading what I would see from there. Two girls against the Commandante and scores of soldiers? My throat tightened, and I fought back tears, but kept climbing, the musket knocking hard against my backbone.

Chapter Twenty Five. Meilu and Tabitha On the Rampart

By the time we reach the corner of the castle, Tabitha has regained her feet. She limps beside me. Our eyes yearn for the *Pieces of Eight* as we round the corner. The sight that greets us stops us in our tracks. Below, the *Pieces of Eight* has pulled away from the dock in a smoky haze of battle. The sound and flashes of musket shots raking the ship blanket the dock. The ship, though, seems to barely move in the sultry, still air. On the road below us, we see the Commandante and a knot of soldiers rushing up toward us. He is bellowing for his men on the rampart to raise the chain and prime the Twelve Apostles. To our right, on the rampart, we see men jumping to the task.

Tabitha looks into my eyes, and the world is suddenly clear, and simple. We are dead, caught between the soldiers behind us and the Commandante in front. So be it. Our last task is to save our friends on the ship, and quickly. That means dealing with the Twelve Apostles. The chain. And wind. I can perhaps imagine the first two. But wind for the ship?

My sister slashes the dirk across her palm, drops the red blade into the dust, and raises her bleeding hand to the heavens, leaning her head back.

"*Chango*!" she cries, in a voice I have never heard from her. "*Chango*, you *orisha* of thunder and storms! Hasten your steps, my lord! You are coming. Come faster!"

She is shrieking now, to the skies, as blood runs down her arm and gathers on her shoulder, a twin to my bloody shoulder from the musket ball. "Faster! Come now!!"

As the soldiers behind us round the corner, a cool breeze whips around Tabitha, blowing her torn shirt and black hair. The soldiers abruptly stop, their eyes wide. The breeze intensifies, and Tabitha screams again to the heavens.

"Come, *Chango*! Come!!"

The soldiers are looking around, and up, frightened, as the wind rushes in from the south, and whips up the dust on the road. A sudden crack of thunder booms to the south. The storm is upon us, the smell of rain filling the air.

Below us, the *Pieces of Eight's* sails suddenly billow out, and the ship jerks north, toward the mouth of the bay. It begins to move, slowly, but with gathering momentum.

The Commandante and a score of men make the last turn in the road and are before us. He jerks to a sudden stop as he sees us, eyes wide with shock and disbelief.

Tabitha lowers her arms, and retrieves the dirk from the dust, her face aflame with joy at the storm's arrival.

"How?" stammers the Commandante. "But no matter," he says, as he sees his men behind us. "Trapped! You will not escape me now. The black devil and her mongrel friend. I'll shoot you here. Now."

"Our friends will escape," Tabitha hisses at him, hatred in her voice.

"Oh, I think not," the Commandante answers confidently. "Do you see? The Twelve Apostles are being readied. If they escape the cannon, the chain has plenty of time to be raised before they reach it, even in the wind. You, and your friends, are dead. I'll put a pistol to each of your heads, myself, then throw your bodies over the cliff into the bay, to join your friends there." He throws back his head, and laughs, as he reaches for the pistol in his belt.

Tabitha and I are off before his fingers touch the pistol. Dashing to the right, onto the rampart. She leads, having been here and done this before. She slashes her dirk into the midst of the two soldiers at the first cannon, who fall back. I shove my torch into the cannon's fuse, and before we are halfway to the second Apostle the first one has fired, sending its cruel load of nails, chain, and shot far to the front of the *Pieces of Eight* sailing by.

The same with the second and third Apostles. The next several are not yet primed, so Tabitha vaults the cannon and kicks the bucket of powder, spilling it along the ground. I stab my torch into the black mess, and we leave half a dozen walls of flame behind us as we race down the rampart.

I vaguely am aware of the Commandante's furious shouts behind us, but am much too busy to take any satisfaction. Tabitha and I are dodging, twisting, whirling our dirk and torch to cut a path through the men around the cannons. I notice the *Pieces of Eight* below us is not moving as fast as we are, but is making progress toward the mouth of the bay–and the chain.

My torch has burned out, so I fling it at the next group of soldiers, and Tabitha and I knock over the buckets of cannister shot as we vault the cannon. Only one cannon left, and beyond it the great gear wheels of the chain. A dozen soldiers are pushing the massive wooden capstan around, moving the first gear wheel which meshes with the second one that is reeling in the chain.

I see that much of the chain is already on the wheel. I glance to my left, into the bay far below, and my heart sinks. The chain is visible, perhaps only ten feet below the surface. But the men are still pushing the capstan, so there must be more to be lifted.

I glance back at Tabitha, and jerk my head toward the dozen men pushing the capstan. It seems impossible to me. She shakes her head, and dashes ahead of me.

"Do as I do," she yells hoarsely as she passes.

She vaults the barrel of the last cannon, and rather than scattering the bucket of cannister shot, she picks it up with a grunt. I'm close behind her, and grab another bucket of shot there. The buckets are very heavy with their load of iron, and we lurch awkwardly with them.

She hurries not to the capstan, but to the spot where the two gear wheels mesh together. One is being pushed by the soldiers, the other reeling in the chain, in a grinding, groaning meeting of the two sets of cogs. She rushes up and with a grunt lifts her bucket of nails, chains, and shot into the air above the confluence of the two wheels. She upends the bucket. The pieces of iron rain down on the meshing cogs, and they begin to catch between the wheels. She drops the bucket itself into the wheels.

I see what she is doing, and quickly add my load of iron to the mix. As we watch, before our eyes the iron nails and chains infiltrate the gear and with a horrible, grating noise the two meshing cogs slow and then, filled with the extra metal, the gears freeze up and the wheels stop. Push as they may, the men cannot raise the chain further, until the dozens of pieces of iron are cleaned from the gears.

A rain of musket shots ricochet off the great wheels, and we remember the Commandante and our pursuers. We crouch low, crawl under the gears, and emerge into the last stretch of the rampart. No cannons, no gear wheels, just fifty yards of dust and weeds–then the low stone wall at the cliff, and the sea beyond, two hundred feet down.

Our legs will barely obey us, our lungs are burning. We stumble and drag ourselves to the sea wall, pushed more by the shouts and musket balls of the Commandante's men behind us, than by our own muscles. Ahead of us is the sea, a deep turquoise impossibly far below us. We turn, and hold each other's hand as the soldiers swarm nearer to us. Tabitha holds her dirk in front of us in a last show of resistance, but has no strength left, and it drops into the dust from her numb, shaking hand.

The men stop some dozen yards from us, and stare in silence, breathing hard. We are a sight, I know. Bleeding, me from my shoulder, my sister from her hand. Clothes in rags, from the jumping and vaulting and slipping and falling. Powder smudges from the fires we have started. But we are proud. Defiant. Emerged from our chrysalis, we are steel butterflies, that sting. We dare them to come closer, and they do not. They are waiting for their leader.

The Commandante arrives, looking little better than us. His once-white uniform is soiled and torn. His handsome face is contorted in fury and fatigue. His men melt away from us as he places himself directly before us. We back away, until our calves are pressed against the rough stones of the low sea wall.

"You are...amazing," he concedes, breathing heavily. "But you cannot escape me. You have failed."

"No!" Tabitha spits out. "The ship will soon pass us. Your cannons were useless against it. Look at them. They are pitiful."

In spite of himself, the Commandante turns around, and views the long row of carnage we have caused. Shot scattered everywhere, fires of powder still burning on the ground, the great frozen gear wheels.

"It will be repaired, and cleaned," he wheezes. "But the chain was already raised. The ship will founder on it."

"I don't know, Commandante," comes the voice of Lieutenant Sanchez. "I'm not so sure."

With a snarl the Commandante turns on his lieutenant, who is staring at the *Pieces of Eight* sailing quickly up to the chain below us. Soon we are all fixed on the ship, not fifty feet from the sea wall and us, and less than that from the chain. We can see and hear everything on the ship, including Silver's booming voice.

"To the stern, me lads!" he is roaring. "Grab some weight and to the rear, double quick, me stalwarts. Everyone to the stern!"

We watch, with unbelieving eyes, soldiers and girls and Commandante, as the crew streams to the rear of the ship, carrying anything they can lay hands to. Soon Silver on the poop deck is the most forward hand, the wheel in his hands, bellowing orders, his eyes aflame.

His intent is soon clear. The extra weight in the rear lifts the bow of the ship, and it slides up to and onto the chain with a terrible grating noise of copper on steel. The copper hull of the ship doesn't clear the chain but rather rides it, grinding over it, lifting the bow even higher in the water amidst the grating clash of metal on metal. Not a soul breathes as the ship hangs in the middle atop the chain, then its momentum pushes it over the chain, and the bow plunges down on the other side. With a furious bucking movement the ship is over the chain and surging through the sea nearly beside us.

Our friends have escaped!

A few involuntary cheers erupt from the soldiers, which quickly die as the Commandante whirls on them, snarling and trembling in his fury. In a second he has whirled back to us, and drawn his pistol from his belt–double-barreled, I note. Two shots. For my sister and me. Our friends are safe, so my heart is proud. Pan Fulong will be proud of me.

"This is all due to you two, black devil and mongrel."

So saying he raises his pistol and cocks the hammers, aiming the first barrel at Tabitha. We glance quickly at each other, eyes unafraid, and then defiantly stare straight at the pistol, not a yard from our faces.

The shot rings out. Strange, the noise seems to come from our right. We look right. There, in plain view, is the foremast of the *Pieces of Eight* sailing past, and Jim Hawkins kneeling in the crows nest, nearly at our level. Hawkins is holding a musket at his shoulder, out of whose barrel smoke is curling. I follow the line of the barrel, which leads straight to–the Commandante.

The Commandante sways. A red spot is blooming in the middle of his chest. His hand holding the pistol sags, and falls to his side. Then the Commandante sags also, and crumples at our feet.

We look back to Jim Hawkins. He is standing now in the crows nest, one hand clutching the mast, the other holding the musket loosely at his side. The wind blows his blonde hair, and we see an easy grin come to his sunburned face. With a jolt it strikes me how handsome he looks, something I've never noticed before.

Our eyes meet. My face is burning. Suddenly I understand why I was so dazed at his touch earlier.

I see him mouth a word to me, rather than hear him.

"Come," he says, with another grin. His face is like a blessing to me. My heart soars. The world is perfect.

Then he is gone, as the *Pieces of Eight* sweeps by us.

Silence at the sea wall. Nothing but the wind. Large drops of rain begin to fall, splattering around us. The men are all staring down at the Commandante's body.

Lieutenant Sanchez shuffles up to it, and pushes his foot against it. Mud is beginning to stain the soiled white uniform, as the rain splashes down heavier now.

"He's dead," he says in a hollow voice.

More silence. No one moves. It is raining hard, now, and the wind is pushing out to sea.

Sanchez sighs, heavily. "I regret I must take you to the dungeons. Both of you," he says to us, in a voice almost apologetic.

"I don't think so," I answer. "I'll take my chances with *Ma Tsu* and the sea."

I turn, and step quickly onto the sea wall.

Tabitha is beside me, in an instant. "To *Chango*, and the wind!" she shouts, her eyes dancing.

I take her hand, and we leap out into the air. Two butterflies, taking flight. The sea seems to hang far below us for a second, then begins to rush up towards us, wondrously fast. All is wind and sea and the salt air, clean and pure.

"*Ma Tsu*," I yell, joyously.

"*Chango*, and *Obatala*!" my sister answers.

We fly. Steel butterflies that sting.

Chapter Twenty Six. The Elixir of Life

The stars gleam above us, brighter than I have ever seen from Grandfather's courtyard in Havana. Leaning on the railings, we can see the *cocullos* flashing their lights on the shore. After the tumult of the day–the escape from the castle, our flight along the rampart, being fished battered but alive from the sea by Hawkins and Silver–the night's calm seems other-worldly.

Yet here we are, on the *Pieces of Eight*, watching the coast slip by on our way to Punta Gorda and the Vinales Valley.

"You could not leave the Commandante for Silver or me, could you?" Tabitha says with mock indignation to Hawkins.

We all laugh.

"Seemed like the thing to do, at the moment," he answers. "In truth, it was a very lucky shot. The crows nest was heaving."

"For meself, I forgives you, Jim Hawkins," says Silver expansively. "I'm just glad to see the rat gone."

"I think you'll have to leave the island, and quickly," I say to Silver.

He laughs, and takes a draw on a cigar he has lit to celebrate our escape, a gift from Grandfather. I notice Hawkins positioning himself upwind from the cigar.

"Ye won't find it hard to believe, me friends, but the Commandante were no more loved by many others than he were by us," answers Silver. Another draw on the cigar, whose end glows in the dark.

"My old friend from Lagos Island, Governor-General Cacigal, in particular will not be mourning the loss of the Commandante," Silver adds. "Oh, he'll regret the *misunderstandings* that led to the *disturbances*. But he's already got the next harbor-master tabbed, and I 'spect that if I lay low for half a year, things will blow over."

"So you and Lady Silver will stay at Vinales Valley, Long John?" Hawkins asks.

Silver nods, savoring the cigar. "Aye, and I thinks I'll start manufact'ring me own cigars at the plantation from me tobaccy there. No sense letting others make the high profits from cigars."

He casts a sharp look at the three of us. "I'd be might happy to have any or all of ye join me and the missus there, if ye'd a mind. We'll need quick hands and smart heads."

A silence descends upon us. Hawkins speaks up first.

"Long John, I'd be happy to build a place of my own next to yours. But mainly I want to be at sea. You know how I feel about the wind in my sails, the smell of salt air, bare feet on a wood deck."

We all nod, recognizing that feeling in ourselves.

"I've a mind to start a trading company," Hawkins plunges on. "I'll carry your cigars and whatever else I can get from Cuba to the other islands, Long John, and to Savannah. Buy and sell. Whatever it takes to keep me on a ship."

"By thunder, I'll lay to it you'll be a rip-roaring trader," Silver says, slapping the rail with his free hand. "Ye can have this here *Pieces of Eight* and the crew for your voyages, me lad. It's time I be spending more o' me days with my missus, anyway."

"Why, thank you, Long John," Hawkins says, putting a hand on the other's shoulder. "I'll pay you handsomely for the use of your ship."

I stare at Hawkins hand on Silver's shoulder. I remember how my skin burned when he touched me before I left for the castle.

"Hawkins. I have a suggestion for your first voyage," I say quietly.

He turns his eyes to me, intrigued. "Yes?"

"Our holds here on the *Pieces of Eight* are bursting with treasure from ancient China," I point out. "It will take some time for us to sort through it all–choose what we want to keep for ourselves. That new home of yours near Long John and Lady Silver's will be gorgeously decorated. As will Grandfather's home, from his share. But after that, what's left over–the best market for it will be China. China, by far."

Silver's laugh fills the night air. "By the powers, Jim lad, Meilu's assigning you the China run for your first voyage! Around the horn of South America, and cross the whole bloody Pacific! Can you imagine?"

My heart lifts, as a smile comes to Hawkins lips. I had not noticed before, but they are beautiful, full and expressive.

"Yes. Yes, I can imagine that, Long John," he says. "You and your Tanka crew will sail your seagoing junk alongside me, Meilu, showing me the way?"

I stare into his eyes. "Yes. I'd like that, Hawkins. And I'd like your help, in facing my reception from Madame Pan in Shanghai. It will be–interesting."

"I'm already looking forward to it," Hawkins says, the smile still on his lips.

I look over to my sister. "You will join us, Tabitha? I can't imagine facing Madame Pan without you at my side."

Tabitha's white teeth shine in the darkness, lit by the glow of Silver's cigar. "On one condition," she answers.

"What?"

Tabitha looks around, to see we're alone. "Promise me Isaiah will be on one ship or the other," she whispers.

Laughter all around.

Long John throws his cigar over the side. We watch its glow sail down to the water, then disappear. "Stay here, me hearties, while I grabs something below," he says in a mysterious tone.

When he returns, he is carrying a lantern, in whose light he places an object on the top of the apple barrel, and pulls four glasses from his pockets. The object glows, throwing off sparks of gold. It is the golden flask from *Ma Tsu's* altar in the sea cave.

"We're all a'hatching big plans, it seems," Long John says. "Strikes me, by thunder, that we could make use of some help the good lady in the sea cave offered us."

Long John twists and removes the top of the golden flask.

"Meilu," he says. "What says the inscription, again?"

I lean into the light of the lantern, and read the characters, carved in gold centuries ago in my homeland, on the other side of the world.

"Life is splendid, throwing off bright rays of joy and sorrow, beauty and ugliness, light and dark, in the dance of being. Accept it all. Not wishing to change the flow of the Tao, we may yet wish to respectfully prolong our days of the dance. This elixir invigorates the ch'i and maintains the balance of yin and yang, so your days are without number, and the dance stretches far into the unseen future. Long life!"

We contemplate it in silence for some moments.

"What's the elixir made of?" Hawkins wonders.

I shrug. "Herbs. Minerals. Parts of plants and animals. Things full of life and *ch'i* energy. The recipe has been a closely guarded secret, for many thousands of years."

Satisfied, Hawkins takes the golden goblet in his strong hands, and pours from it into the four glasses. The liquid is golden, like the goblet itself–like life itself.

Four hands reach for the glasses, and lift them into the air. High.

Tabitha and I glance at each other. Steel butterflies, that sting. Young women, dreaming of our future, imagining adventures and lovers. Our faces are smiling and bright in the lantern light. Eager for the future. For the dance. For the wind in our sails and the freedom of the sea.

"*Long life*!" we all shout, together, and the elixir is in us.

Note on Sources

1. The backbone and back story of *The Return to Treasure Island* is, of course, the original 1883 *Treasure Island*, by Robert Louis Stevenson. My son and I reverently read aloud the 1920 edition by Scribner many years ago. More accessible to modern tastes is the masterful 1996 Viking edition, with gorgeous watercolor illustrations by Francois Place.

No offense to RLS, who created an enduring masterpiece of pirates and young boys, but in places the story drags. And of course–there's hardly a female character!

The 1950 Walt Disney movie with Robert Newton solves the first weakness, and in fact is probably the version of *Treasure Island* most adults today fell in love with as kids.

The Return to Treasure Island solves the second weakness, by incorporating two strong young females into the Treasure Island saga.

2. Havana's colorful and exotic past is captured well in Juliet Barclay's *Havana–Portrait of a City* (1993, Cassell, London). Ms. Barclay examines the city's art, architecture, and social life from its beginnings to the nineteenth century in clear prose with many lavish illustrations and photos. I have incorporated many features, large and small, into my story.

3. The evidence for a great Chinese fleet of Ming dynasty treasure ships circumnavigating the world in 1421 is presented in Gavin Menzies' fascinating and controversial best-seller *1421–the Year China Discovered*

America (2003, HarperCollins, New York). Menzies places the ships under Admiral Zhou Wen sailing into the Caribbean and along the north coast of Cuba before veering up the eastern coast of North America. He thinks it likely that many of those ships foundered on the infamous Bahama Bank along Cuba's north coast, and presents evidence of such happenings.

If Menzies' proposals are true, then it follows that a Chinese colony and some of the cargo of the treasure ships would have been left in the Caribbean, probably in Cuba. I predicate such in *The Return to Treasure Island.*

It should be noted that the claims made in Menzies' book are apparently widely accepted in China, both popularly and in the scholarly community, and have been for some time. In the West, his proposals have not been welcomed by the scholarly community. His evidence is for the most part circumstantial, and Western historians demand much more in terms of evidence and support for a thesis.

I make no claims that Menzies' claims are true or established. I merely use them to create an interesting and plausible fictional story.

4. The ancient cult of the sea-goddess *Ma Tsu* is widespread in southern coastal China, in Taiwan, and in Chinese settlements throughout Southeast Asia, even today. I have lit incense in many of her shrines there. Discussion of the cult can be found in Robert van Gulick's *Sexual Life in Ancient China*, Kristopher Schipper's *The Taoist Body*, and Isabelle Robinette's *A Brief History of the Taoist Religion.*

5. Online researches of various internet sites gave me my material on the slave trade in the Gulf of Niger, the Benin Bight, and the Yoruba people's society and religion of *orisha*. The Caribbean evolution of aspects of that religion into *Santeria* is discussed also in Barclay's book on Havana.

6. The famous 18th century *bon vivant* Samuel Johnson was a lexicographer as well as a critic. I have taken the liberty of inventing a definition by him of *chrysalis*, given on the page preceding the list of chapters. Perhaps it even exists–though I have not yet found it in the records. The Michael Chabon

quote there is from the Afterword of his dazzling *Gentlemen of the Road* (2007). The quote, and the accompanying discussion in the Afterword, neatly captures the universal yearning for adventure, and the pleasures of partaking in it, even vicariously.

7. My chief source of information on the city of Havana was my old Chico friend (and 21st century *bon vivant*) Rudy Giscombe, who has sailed into Cuba on several occasions taking photographs for his excellent exhibitions of images from contemporary Havana. His generous and convivial conversations and use of his books and maps are much appreciated and gratefully acknowledged.

About the Author

Raymond Barnett studied Chinese history and language at Yale University, where he graduated Magna cum Laude. After serving in the U.S. Army in Vietnam, he earned his Ph.D. in biology from Duke University and taught biology at California State University, Chico for three decades. He was instrumental in the founding of the Gateway Science Museum there, for which he was named "The Father of the Museum" by the museum Board.

Barnett cultivated his interest in the Far East during his biology career, traveling extensively in China, Taiwan, Japan, and Korea, and writing the historical novel *Jade and Fire* (published by Random House) and the Taoism primer *Relax, You're Already Home: everyday Taoist habits for a richer life* (published by Penguin/Putnam). Since his retirement in 2003, Barnett has written *The China Ultimatum*, a thriller set in the near future, and *The Return to Treasure Island*, a novel set in 18th century Cuba (both published by iUniverse).

For relaxation, Barnett enjoys backpacking in the Sierra Nevada high country, snorkeling in Hawaii, and bicycling in Chico. Further information and slides of his travels can be found on his website, www.raymondbarnett.com.